FRIEND OR FICTION

FRiEND OR FiCTiON

Abby Cooper

Charlesbridge

For Michael

Published by Charlesbridge
85 Main Street
Watertown, MA 02472
(617) 926-0329
www.charlesbridge.com

Library of Congress Cataloging-in-Publication Data
Names: Cooper, Abby, author.
Title: Friend or fiction / Abby Cooper.
Description: Watertown, MA : Charlesbridge, [2019] | Summary: "In the pages
    of her notebook, soon after her father is diagnosed with cancer, Jade invents
    an imaginary best friend she can depend on—Zoe; but when Zoe somehow
    magically shows up in real life, Jade wonders how genuine their friendship
    can possibly be if Jade's controlling Zoe through what she writes in her
    notebook"—Provided by publisher.
Identifiers: LCCN 2018058502 (print) | LCCN 2019001366 (ebook) | ISBN
    9781632898708 (ebook) | ISBN 9781623541088 (reinforced for library use)
Subjects: LCSH: Imaginary companions—Juvenile fiction. | Best friends—
    Juvenile fiction. | Friendship—Juvenile fiction. | Magic—Juvenile fiction. |
    Imagination—Juvenile fiction. | Fathers and daughters—Juvenile fiction. |
    Children of cancer patients—Juvenile fiction. | CYAC: Imaginary playmates—
    Fiction. | Best friends—Fiction. | Friendship—Fiction. | Magic—Fiction. |
    Imagination—Fiction. | Fathers and daughters—Fiction. | Cancer—Fiction.
Classification: LCC PZ7.1.C6477 (ebook) | LCC PZ7.1.C6477 Fr 2019 (print) | DDC
    813.6 [Fic]—dc23
LC record available at https://lccn.loc.gov/2018058502

Printed in the United States of America
(hc) 10 9 8 7 6 5 4 3 2 1

Display type set in Yellow Gold by Creativeqube Design and Frogster by Typotheticals
Text type set in Constantia by Microsoft Corporation
Printed by Berryville Graphics in Berryville, Virginia, USA
Production supervision by Brian G. Walker
Designed by Diane M. Earley

The Blank Page

OPPSERVATION: You can love something but not really like it very much.

Questions for further research: Why, lunchtime, *why?*

I tucked my oppservation journal into my bag and scanned the cafeteria. This was supposed to be the best part of the day. At least for most people it was. Most people grabbed their lunches as fast as they could and went to their tables with their best friends to laugh and talk and make plans for after school. Most people got to forget about anything bad and just relax and hang out and eat.

Sometimes, during the time it took me to get my brown bag out of my locker and sit at my table, I got sad.

1

But then, once I sat down, I remembered. I was going to have lunch with my best friend, too, just like everybody else. Only my best friend wasn't like anyone else's. She was better.

I sat in my usual spot, took out my cheese sandwich and my yellow notebook, and waited. Sometimes she showed up right away. Other times she took a little longer. Today must have been one of those other times, because it felt like she was taking forever.

I thought about what we might do when she finally got here. After eating, maybe we'd share my headphones and listen to music the way Nia and Zara always do. Or maybe we'd purposely give ourselves milk mustaches and take really funny selfies like Molly and Casey do. We could even do some things that other people around here couldn't, too, like make plans for the weekend. And next weekend. And next year. People in Tiveda, Colorado moved away all the time. I've heard adults call this place a *transient* town, which must mean it's not good enough to stay, or something, because you never really knew who would be at school on Monday and who would've moved on to a new town. But Zoe was always a sure thing. Not only did we have today together, we had all our tomorrows too.

Still, there was a pang deep down in the pit of my stomach as I watched everybody else having fun. For a second I thought Nia and Zara were going to invite me to come sit with them, but then they looked away. I frowned at my notebook. What was taking Zoe so long?

Mrs. Yang, my English teacher, always says that the hardest part is starting. No matter how long you've been writing or how much you love it, she says, sometimes the blank page can be the scariest thing there is. She says that you should just put a word on it. Any word. Then put another one.

I opened my notebook.

Zoe and Jade and the Best Lunch Ever, I wrote at the top. Eight words! Take that, blank page.

I stopped staring at Nia and Zara and Molly and Casey. I took a deep breath. I wrote more. I took a bite of sandwich. I kept going until the warning bell rang, and when it did, I barely even noticed. In my story Zoe and I had just finished taking our milk-mustache selfies and now we were making origami napkin birds for each other. She was drawing funny faces on them and pretending hers were talking, and I was trying to make mine talk back but I couldn't because I was laughing too hard.

When I finally closed my notebook and gathered my stuff, I noticed all the faces looking my way. As bad as blank pages were, blank stares were even worse. My pale skin felt as red as my hair. Yeah, I wrote during lunch. So what? It was pretty obvious by the looks I got that people thought it was weird that my nose was always buried in my notebook. But the one thing they never did was ask.

That was fine, though. I didn't want to tell anybody what I was writing anyway. Out of the corner of my eye, I peeked at Gresham Gorham—or Clue, as everybody called him. It was bad enough that *he* knew my secret.

As if he could feel me looking, Clue turned and stared me right in the face. His dark, serious eyes dropped to my notebook. Then they flashed back to the one in his lap.

My heartbeat quickened, so I took a few long breaths. I pushed my purple glasses up higher on my nose and hugged my notebook to my chest. That calmed me down right away, same as it always did. Forget Clue. Forget other people. Forget everything.

I had Zoe.

And that was all that mattered.

The Beginning of Zoe

2

When I started fourth grade my best friend was Joslin. We'd just moved from Nevada and she'd introduced herself to me right away and everything was awesome. She taught me how to play tetherball without getting hit in the face, and we had nine amazing days of not-getting-hit-in-the-face best-friend fun.

Then she moved away, and I never heard from her again. I kept sending letters, and she kept not writing back.

So then I hung out with Rosie. Rosie liked to write, like me.

But not enough, I guess. After she moved she didn't write letters or emails or postcards like she promised she would. Not even one. And no texts either. But I guess I can't blame her, because I was still the only kid in my grade (and the world, it felt like) who didn't have a cell phone.

I hadn't been in Tiveda for that long, but I was already sick of people coming and going so much. People only lived here so they could feel like they were living in Denver, even though they weren't living in Denver. When they could afford something nicer (usually in Denver), they left.

Sometimes, if they couldn't afford something nicer—or if they couldn't even afford it here—they'd move further down the road, to Bertsburg, where everyone lived in trailers. It wasn't far away, but far enough where the people who lived there went to another school, which may as well have been a whole different universe.

Dad always compared Tiveda to those rest stops in random places off the highway. People pulled over when they needed to stretch their legs, to have a bathroom break and a snack, and then they took off. That's what we were supposed to do while Mom painted murals in buildings around town and

Dad consulted with an energy company, whatever that meant.

But instead of a stretch and a snack, we stayed in Tiveda for a full night of sleep and a full day of meals. Over and over and over again. As U-Hauls pulled in and pulled out, we stayed right where we were. And now we were officially stuck in a town that had a different mailman every other day, three stores that were considered the mall, and zero flowers because whenever anybody planted some, they left when the seeds needed care the most.

In my opinion you should be able to know the name of the person delivering your mail. Three stores did *not* make a mall. And was it really that hard to stay long enough for a flower to bloom?

Because of all this, I was about to give up on ever having a best friend when Vanessa joined my always-changing little class toward the end of fourth grade. Her smile was warm and friendly. Plus she had a giant collection of candles that she really wanted to show off, and I really wanted to see something besides all my own junk. She invited me over right away, and soon we had an after-school tradition every day—to just hang out. Sometimes we'd spend hours lining up the candles from favorite to least favorite. Or most smelly to least smelly. Or tallest to shortest. We never ran out of ways.

Nessa was planning a gigantic birthday party—well, as gigantic as you could get around here—and I helped her get everything ready. It was going to be at one of those places where the whole room was a big trampoline. I had never been to a place like that before, and it sounded totally amazing. And it was only fifteen minutes away, so maybe we could go back sometime. Every day after school we would cross a day off her cute dog calendar. Everything was about jumping and candles and best-friend fun. Everything was fun at home too. Dad was happy. Mom was happy. My little brother Bo was only three, so he was extra cute and hilarious. We were supposed to move soon, too, to a more forever kind of place in Denver. Maybe we'd even get a dog.

So that's why it was a pretty big surprise when Mom and Bo picked me up from the birthday party five minutes after Nessa's parents brought us there.

"We have to go to the hospital," Mom said in a loud, scared voice, the kind that made all the trampoline-jumping people stop and stare.

I hadn't even finished taking off my shoes.

"Why?" I asked. "What's going on?"

"I'll explain in the car," she said. "Go say goodbye to your friends."

Somehow I made my way over to Nessa, even though my legs felt like noodles and my stomach had leapt to my throat.

"I have to go," I said. My voice barely eked out. "I don't know why."

Nessa made a face like she'd just taken a bite of birthday cake, only to discover it was really a sour lemon. "What do you mean?"

I couldn't see Mom from where I was standing, but I could definitely hear her foot tapping by the door. *Let's go*, the taps said. They came faster and louder. *Let's gooooooooo!*

"My mom says I have to," I told Nessa. "Something about the hospital."

Cold air blasted through the room. Nessa frowned. "I don't get it."

I swallowed hard. I felt ice-sculpture frozen.

"Me either."

I waited for her to give me a hug or tell me to call her later or something, because we were best friends, and I obviously didn't *want* to go, and my leaving was bugging both of us and freaking us both out.

But she didn't do any of that. Instead she crossed her arms and said, "Best friends do not miss each other's parties."

"I know!" My voice switched from shaky to shrieky. "I don't want to! But—"

"Jade," Mom called. "Now, please."

My body tensed. It felt like everyone there was jumping on my heart like it was one of the trampolines.

"I—" I couldn't find the right words. I couldn't find *any* words, period. And it didn't matter anyway. Because Nessa—my very best friend in the whole world—had walked away.

Leaving the party barely felt real. Neither did getting in the car, putting on my seatbelt, or driving to the hospital.

Mom said a lot of words in the car, but they all blurred together. Sick. Dad. Tests. Urgent. *Sickdadtestsurgent.* They sounded like one big, blobby word, and my heart felt like a big, blobby mess.

How was it possible that your whole family could be so happy, and everything could be going so well, and you could even be thinking about getting a dog, and then, just like that, you weren't?

And how could a best friend who's supposed to

care about you not understand that something bad was happening, and leaving her party wasn't your choice?

When we got to the hospital, Dad was taking a test that we couldn't help with, so we went to the gift shop instead of to his room. Bo got a sketch pad and crayons and I got the biggest yellow notebook I'd ever seen in my life. Mom looked pretty happy about that. She knew how fast I could fill a regular-sized notebook. There were tons of them piled up in my room already. When you want to be an author some-day, you have to practice a lot.

On the first page of the notebook, I wrote some of the things I'd been thinking about in the car on the way over. I put *Oppservations* at the top. This was the beginning of my list of observations about something opposite, like how your best friend could suddenly become not so friendly when you did some-thing she didn't like, even if it wasn't your fault.

On the next page, I started writing a story. About me and Nessa and trampolines and how things should have gone.

Dad should have been fine. I should have gotten to stay at the party. We should have had the best time ever. Joslin and Rosie should have written to me to apologize for not staying in touch. If I couldn't stay at the party, and Dad wasn't fine, then all my friends, especially Nessa, should have come to the hospital with me. Or called to check on things, or promised to come by later with leftover cake.

Or waved.

Or *something*.

Maybe Nessa wasn't the perfect best friend, even though we always had fun together. And Rosie and Joslin definitely weren't the perfect best friend, because they left me, and they didn't keep in touch, even when I tried to.

I turned the page and started a new story.

Maybe there wasn't a perfect best friend out there for me. Maybe I'd be better off if I created my own.

So instead of writing the names of anyone I knew, I wrote the name *Zoe*.

We finally got to see Dad an hour later, but it wasn't him, not really. The guy in the bed was frowning instead of smiling. His hair stood straight up like he was an actor at Tiveda's Halloween haunted house. His face was white, almost like a ghost's, and he looked fragile, like you could poke him and he'd break. Plus, his arms were attached to all these long, twisty wires. And instead of his typical flannel shirts and tennis shoes, he wore a crinkly paper gown and silly-looking socks. I didn't know who this person was, but it definitely wasn't the dad I knew.

"What are you holding, Jadey?"

He sounded like a different person too.

But at least he could talk. When I tried to make words come out of my mouth, they just sounded like pathetic little squeaks. Mom squeezed my hand, but I couldn't bring myself to squeeze back.

"You writing a story?" the-guy-they-said-was-Dad asked.

Somehow I nodded.

"Read it to me."

I let out the humongous breath I'd been holding since we stepped into the room. No matter what was going on with Dad—like if he was busy or tired or hungry or cranky or sick, like he was now—he knew how much I loved writing stories, and he always wanted to hear one. This stranger really was my dad. I didn't know how to feel about that, so I did the only thing I could: I read.

Sometimes days can trick you. They seem regular, but then, all of a sudden, they're not. My voice shook at first but went back to normal when I saw that Dad was smiling. Jade thought it was a normal Sunday, but when she peeked out the window and saw a girl who looked about her age moving into the house across the street, she had a feeling that everything was about to change. Right away Jade knew there was something different about the girl. Maybe it was the way she raced in circles around her driveway, like being outside was the greatest thing to ever happen to her. Maybe it was the way she put big red stickers that spelled her name on the mailbox, even though people usually put their last names on mailboxes, if they bothered to at all. When Jade met the girl at school on Monday, she knew that her life was about to get much more exciting. Mailbox stickers were only the beginning.

I paused and peeked at Dad again. Maybe I was imagining it, but his face looked a lot less ghost-y. It was even starting to look sort of normal.

I kept going.

The girl, Zoe, had olive skin, long dark hair, bright green eyes, and a heart-shaped birthmark above her left eyebrow. The second she came into Jade's classroom, Jade could tell that Zoe would be super popular. She walked and smiled like someone who would do anything for the people she cared about, like she was awesome, and she knew it. It was like she'd strolled right out of one of those pop songs where the singers encourage people to be strong and powerful. Wherever she went, invisible glitter and confetti followed.

But even in a whole classroom full of people staring at her with please-be-my-friend looks on their faces, it was as if Jade was the only one Zoe could see. She gave Jade this look that said *we are going to be best friends forever and ever and ever no matter what.* And when the teacher let Zoe choose where she wanted to sit, she went straight to the desk next to Jade's, even though there were way better open seats, like the one close to the window and the one with the little bar under it for your feet.

Jade watched as Zoe took out two sparkly blue pencils and set them on her desk. Zoe liked to have a spare, just like Jade did. In fact Jade had two of the same pencils on her desk. When Zoe looked over and noticed this, they giggled so hard that their teacher asked them to please go out into the hallway until they could calm themselves down.

Jade grinned through her laughter. She'd never been in trouble before, but today it didn't seem so bad. Nothing did.

"I'm Zoe, by the way," Zoe said to Jade once they caught their breath in the hall.

"I know, the teacher just introduced you. I'm Jade."

"I know," said Zoe.

"How?" asked Jade.

"Because you just told me!"

They got the giggles all over again. Jade had the feeling it might be a while before they calmed themselves down enough to go back into the room. And that feeling was the best one she'd ever had.

I stopped reading and looked at Dad again. His eyes were closed but he seemed calm, almost happy. His stomach rose and fell with every steady in-and-out breath. For a minute it felt like maybe we could still get that dog after all.

"Do you feel better?" I asked.

Dad opened his eyes. "Sure do," he said.

Maybe I felt better too.

I knew my story wasn't the cure for whatever was wrong with Dad or anything. It wasn't medicine. It couldn't actually have made him better. But what if it did, somehow?

What if Zoe did?

I'd written a ton of stories in my life, but none

like this. There was something different about Zoe. And I knew, right there in the hospital room, this character was here to stay.

Still, that Monday at school, I tried to talk to Nessa.

"I didn't want to leave," I reminded her. "My dad is sick," I said. "You're still important to me."

But Nessa made that same sour face and walked away. Again.

A couple weeks later, she moved to Ohio.

It would have been nice to make up. To somehow stay friends. But that wasn't how things worked for me. Even if we had made up, we probably wouldn't have kept in touch. Maybe we'd promise to write or call, but it would never actually happen. It was fine, though. I didn't need her anyway.

Because I had created Zoe.

3
More Than Zero

The lunch-is-over bell rang. Still clutching my notebook, I tossed my brown bag in the trash and headed toward health class. All the sixth graders at Tiveda Middle had to take health. So far it was pretty *ugh*, but at least I'd had a great lunch, minus the weird part at the end when Clue was looking at me. It was so unfair. Clue didn't deserve to know that I wrote about Zoe. Especially not after what he'd done back in December. I tried to ignore him and focus on getting to my next class, where I could plan more stories.

Maybe tomorrow I'd write one where Zoe and I put on a show with our origami birds. It'd be the funny kind of show, where we're total dorks but know it. Maybe after school or over the weekend, I'd write a story where we make a video of it and put it online, and it goes viral and we get famous and go on a world tour with private helicopters and limos and everything. Or maybe I'd just write about us hanging out with Dad. Now that it was finally spring, maybe we'd all sit on the steps outside and enjoy some nice March air. We didn't always have to do something exciting to have fun and be best friends. Some of my favorite times with Zoe were the ones where we didn't really do anything at all.

"Word count?" Mrs. Yang stood outside her door, like she did every day after lunch. Her dark, shiny hair swished around her as she smiled, first at me, then at my notebook.

"More than zero," I said. If you could have a secret handshake that was made out of words instead of movements, that would be ours. Mrs. Yang knew I wrote at lunch, and she always checked in about it. There wasn't a certain number of words I was supposed to get or anything. As long as my answer was more than zero, that was all that mattered to her. It was funny how people could be interested in my words in different ways. Dad wanted to know what they said. Mrs. Yang just wanted to know that they existed. *Never stop*, she'd say. *When the writing gets hard, remember why you're doing it, and keep going.*

"Any new Oppservations?" she asked next.

"Lunch," I said. "I love it, but sometimes I don't like it. At least not until I start writing. Why is that?"

She smiled and said exactly what I knew she would: "Interesting."

I knew by now that Mrs. Yang was never going to answer all of my questions, but I still kept visiting her between classes and after lunch.

At least she thought my Oppservations were cool. She always says that the best writers are the best observers. They see everything, study everything, and wonder about everything. They come up with answers to impossible questions. If I wanted to be an author someday, I had to do all that. And write the words. *And* make the words good enough for Dad—and the rest of the world—to love. No pressure or anything.

I glanced at my notebook.

You can do it, Zoe seemed to say. *I'm here for you.*

I smiled.

"Have a good afternoon." Mrs. Yang waved.

I gave my notebook a little squeeze, and I knew that I would.

4
Out of Sorts

After school I picked Bo up from the elementary school across the street. All three Tiveda schools were on Main Street, which sounded great when I first heard about it. Like I'd be right in the middle of all the exciting town action. It got a lot less awesome when I realized that the only other things on Main Street were the *Tiveda Family Restaurant*, the three-store "mall," a teeny tiny coffee shop, a gas station, a bus stop, and a whole bunch of struggling flowers.

As we walked behind the gas station toward endless rows of boxy little houses, Bo updated me about all the things happening in kindergarten. It was hard to concentrate on his stories when I had so many more of my own I needed to write. The ideas spun around in my mind like clothes in the laundry.

At home Dad sat in his big brown armchair in front of the TV, as usual. His whole face lit up when he saw us, and it got even brighter when he noticed the massive yellow notebook tucked under my arm.

"There are my three favorite kids," he said. I smiled. It was cool how Dad treated Zoe like she was real, like she was such a good friend she was practically part of the family. For a second I almost forgot anything was wrong. But then I saw his hat.

Today Dad was wearing a fake-gold plastic Viking hat with small silver horns poking out the top and long, fake brown hair braided down the sides. Dad caught me noticing and made a face *like you can laugh now*. But the laugh got caught in my throat somewhere and refused to come out.

"You don't like my braids? It took me *all day* to make them look this good." He scrunched his face up like he was deeply offended, and then he winked.

Bo grinned. "I think you look beautiful," he said, "and I'm not even kidding!"

A thin smile crossed my lips. I didn't know why I wasn't laughing; today's hat *was* funny. But there was nothing funny about the fact that Dad was bald underneath. Even though he finished chemo last week—he got an official certificate and everything—it could take a while for his hair to grow back.

It didn't seem like Dad was used to being a baldy, either, which was why he always covered his head with different hats. Sometimes he'd do a regular old baseball hat or one of those big floppy things people wore when it was really sunny, but he usually liked to get creative with it. He must've been feeling extra creative today, because he looked totally ridiculous. And, okay, maybe he looked kind of hilarious too. Finally I let out a little chuckle. Eventually it turned into a full-on laugh.

OPPSERVATION: Some things that are really un-funny can actually be super funny in their un-funniness.

Questions for further research: Why do those things always seem to involve Dad?

He waited for me to finish writing—sometimes I kept my Oppservations in my head, but if I could write them down, I did—then he asked, "So what's new with Zoe?" He wrapped a firm Dad hand around my waist and pulled me closer to his chair.

Bo made a silly face like he did every time Dad brought up Zoe. "You're too big for an imaginary friend," he told me, same as always.

"She's not imaginary," I said. Bo was too young to understand, but Dad did.

"Lunch was so funny," I told him. "We had the best time. In my story we took milk-mustache selfies and made napkin birds."

"Napkin birds!" Dad repeated. "Can they fly like real ones?"

I rolled my eyes, but in a joking way. "Sure," I said. "They can also play fetch, juggle, and do your homework for you."

Bo's blue eyes lit up. "I want to play with those birds!"

Dad nodded. "Me too. They sound pretty talented."

"Right? I might write about using them for my homework tonight." I hoisted my backpack higher and tapped my notebook against my knee.

"I see that twinkle in your eyes." Dad pointed at my face, and I beamed. It wasn't like I could actually see my own eyes or anything, but whenever he pointed out my twinkle, somehow I just knew it was there.

He tickled my arm. "Go ahead," he said. "Go write. I'll be here when you get back."

I knew he would be, since he never really left that chair. And that made me happy and sad at the same time.

≈

A week after Dad went to the hospital for the first time (the day of Nessa's party), Mom sat Bo and me down on the couch and looked at us with a very serious face. Dad sat in the armchair and closed his eyes, and that was when I got the sinking feeling that he might not be getting up anytime soon.

"I know we were just going to make a pit stop here in Tiveda," Mom started, and I waited for her to be like, *Well, it's over! Pack your bags. We're heading somewhere fun where dads don't get sick and best friends don't disappear.*

But that wasn't what she said next.

"We're going to stay a bit longer than we planned. It would just be too hard to move right now."

I squirmed around on the couch. How long were we going to have to stay? No one stayed here that long. We'd probably already set a record.

Mom paced back and forth across the room. "You know Dad hasn't been feeling so great lately," she said. "We need to stay here so the doctors can help him get better." Her voice cracked, but a smile stayed glued to her face. As I looked closer I noticed that Dad wasn't the only one who seemed different. Mom's hair was falling out of her ponytail, and there were weird dark circles under her eyes, like something had gone wrong with her makeup—or maybe with her sleep.

"Dad loves you both very much," she said. "But he might start being out of it a little more. That's part of the process of getting better." As if to prove it, she motioned toward Dad. He had fallen asleep on the chair.

"Being out of *what* a little more?" Bo asked. I looked up, surprised he was even paying attention. He'd been doodling on his Etch A Sketch the whole time.

"Out of . . . sorts," Mom said.

"Oh," said Bo. "I hope he gets his sorts back on."

Mom's feet came to a sudden stop. She and I looked at each other, and we couldn't help but laugh, even with all the weirdness that hung in the air like a storm cloud waiting to burst.

When we were done, Mom's face turned serious.

"He's going to be out of it," she repeated, and I couldn't help but wonder if she was also saying, *I'm going to be out of it too.*

I shifted around on the couch some more. It had always been one of the comfiest places in the whole house, but now I couldn't find a single spot that felt good.

"You two need to be tough, okay?"

I felt Mom's eyes on me, and only me. Why didn't Bo have to be tough?

"You can always come to us for anything, but if you have any problems that you think you might be able to work out on your own, well, it'd be really helpful if you tried."

A lump the size of a notebook formed in my throat. I wrung my hands together, stared at the floor, and thought of about a zillion things I'd been meaning to ask Mom and Dad for help with. I didn't understand my math homework. There was a weird smell coming from my room and I didn't know why. And I'd just lost my best friend, Nessa. I'd been feeling big, confusing feelings about a lot of things, but I didn't know what the feelings were or where they came from. But I guess I'd never know, because now it was too late to ask.

"Don't worry," Mom said. "It's going to be okay."

She lowered herself onto the fat armrest of the chair and put her arm around Sleeping Dad. Bo stopped doodling. He looked my way, but I couldn't quite get my eyes to meet his. Not that the floor was super interesting, but it felt like the only thing I could look at that wouldn't make me burst into tears. Soon enough Bo looked away, grabbed his favorite stuffed animal, Giraffe, and gave him a gigantic hug.

After a few minutes I slowly raised my head. I looked from Mom and Dad to Bo and Giraffe. My arms felt empty. Everybody else's had something to hold. I was with my family, but it felt like I was all by myself.

So I did the only thing I could think of. I picked up my notebook from the floor, wrapped my arms around it, and squished it to my chest. It was probably my imagination, but it kind of felt like it was hugging me back.

Then I started writing a story. It was about Zoe, and how she was just what I needed. With her as a best friend, I'd be way too busy to worry about any of the thoughts and fears buzzing around in my brain like a big swarm of bees.

"I'm scared," I admitted to Zoe once in the story. "I'm really scared."

"It's okay," she told me. "I get it. It's scary. We don't have to talk about it if you don't want to. I'm here no matter what."

"Thanks," I said back.

With Zoe, and with everyone, actually, I decided it was best to not really talk about it.

When I finished my story, I took my notebook and hugged it even tighter.

It had been two years, but I hadn't really let go since.

5

Evaporation

After a busy night of writing and a long morning of school, I got to third-period science on Friday and opened my notebook. Mrs. Yang always said that if I was serious about being an author, I should practice writing every chance I got. After all, she said everything I wrote helped me become a better writer, even if it never got published or shared or anything. Every word mattered.

She probably didn't mean I should practice every chance I got in school, but oh, well. Practice was practice. And I'd paid good attention in my first two classes, for the most part. Besides, Zoe and I were in

the middle of something important in my story, and I couldn't just abandon her. She'd never do that to me.

So, I opened to where I left off and kept going. I made sure to write in my tiniest handwriting, the same way I had since last year when I realized I was writing too much too fast and getting too close to the end of the notebook. I wanted all my Zoe stories in one place. They belonged together, just like Zoe and me.

Jade went up to the room she shared with Bo, where Zoe was waiting for her. They took out their homework and their favorite pencils. They were pretty good at getting ready to do homework. They just weren't always that good at actually doing it.

"Wouldn't that be cool?" Jade asked. "That thing I said to my dad, about birds that could do our homework for us? I wish they were real."

Zoe hadn't been there for that conversation with Jade's dad, but she still knew exactly what Jade was talking about. She always did. She also knew when Jade wanted to talk about something more, and when she didn't. Like now, Jade didn't want to talk about the fact that her dad still had to wear hats to cover up his bald head. She just wanted to talk about birds. And Zoe knew it.

"I wish birds that could do your homework were real too," Zoe said. "I wish they fluttered around and sang happy little bird songs during homework time."

"That sounds like something right out of a homework fairy tale," Jade said.

"And they all lived homework-ly ever after," said Zoe.

They grinned at each other.

"Homework-ly ever aaaaaaafter," Jade sang over and over and over again. It was an off-key song with no real melody, but that didn't stop her from singing it at the top of her lungs.

Zoe did too. Then she got up, flapped her arms, and fluttered around the room. That was the thing about real, true best friends. You could say weird things and be random and sing terrible songs that had only three words. And instead of making fun of you or ditching you, your best friend would keep dancing with you.

Zoe fluttered around the room a few more times until she got tired of dancing and Jade got tired of singing. They flopped onto Jade's bed at the same time.

"I guess we should actually do our homework," Zoe said.

"Probably," Jade agreed. "Goodbye, magical homework birds who don't actually exist."

"Goodbye, beautiful homework-ly ever after fairy tale of fun," said Zoe.

"Goodbye—"

"Jade?"

Goodbye Jade? I didn't know exactly what I was going to write next, but that definitely wasn't it.

I looked up. The "Jade" hadn't come from my brain like the rest of the story. It had come from Mrs. Wilson, who was staring at me like she had been waiting on me for a really long time. I pushed my notebook off my desk into my messenger bag and blinked about a thousand times.

"Do you know the answer to the question, Jade?" Mrs. Wilson asked. She sighed. "I asked for the next step of the water cycle."

Last night I had totally done my homework, once Mom made me stop writing my latest Zoe story. But this water cycle stuff wasn't as memorable as singing or dancing. Or anything I ever did with Zoe, really, even if it was all just happening in my head and in my notebook.

From the seat next to me, Clue made a big display of hiding his face behind his hands and arms. He had a reputation for trying to help people when teachers asked tough questions, which is how he got his nickname. Even though I wasn't going to forgive him for what happened this winter, I was really lucky to have him in so many of my classes. Particularly at this very moment.

"Um . . ." I tried to look like I was thinking while sneakily glancing his way. I watched his long, thinly braided hair and his serious eyes, but I couldn't figure it out. He wiggled his fingers like he was making jazz hands at the sky, and then covered his face again. Dancing? Disappearing inside a dance? A dance that made you disappear?

"Oh!" I had it, finally. I sat up straighter. "Evaporation," I told Mrs. Wilson.

"You got it."

Clue lowered his jazz hands and shot me a smile. Even better than having Clue in my classes was the fact that none of the teachers stopped him, even when he was being really obvious. He never raised his hand or said the answers himself. He just gave them away to other people like little presents.

Mrs. Wilson asked someone else a question, and

I went to the front of the room to sharpen my pencil. It was risky to go back to my story after what had just happened, but I couldn't stop now. I had so much more to write.

I sat down and reached inside my bag when Mrs. Wilson was turned to the board. My hand couldn't seem to find my notebook, which was kind of ridiculous considering how huge it was. I leaned over and rummaged through, but there was only my thin math book, a few extra pencils, an apple, and my very favorite lip balm that was strawberry flavored on one end and watermelon on the other.

No notebook.

I had to stay calm, but my heartbeat quickened, and my breath got caught somewhere deep inside me where it couldn't come out. I took a few fast breaths. It was a *notebook*. It wasn't like it grew feet and got up and walked down the hall to the vending machines for some chips. It wasn't like it joined the water cycle and evaporated. It *had* to be around here somewhere.

Only it wasn't on the floor. It wasn't behind me or in front of me or to the side. It had actually disappeared. I studied Clue. He could definitely be mean, but not in a notebook-thief kind of way. Except my bag was on the floor on the side of my desk closest to his. If anybody had snatched it when I went to sharpen my pencil, he would've seen it happen.

"Have you seen my notebook?" I whispered to Clue.

He just shrugged and made a face I couldn't quite read.

I sucked in a big breath and tried to hold in the tears that were filling the sides of my eyes. That notebook held all of my Zoe stories. Every single one. That notebook—and my ultimate best friend—were everything, and now they were gone.

6
A Blow-your-Mind Surprise

rs. Yang always says that good writers take risks. That they try things even if they're not sure that the things will work out. After all, if something doesn't work, you can cross it out and try it again a different way. But at least you won't be stuck wondering if it could've been better had you just tried the thing you were scared to do.

Maybe this wasn't only true about writing. Maybe it was good to take risks in real life too.

That's why, as Clue gathered his stuff at the end of class, I tapped him on the shoulder, even though it felt about as comfortable as grabbing the pointy end of a pencil. He looked at me, and my breaths turned sharper, quicker, and angrier. We hadn't really looked at each other like this since that time he showed me what a jerk he could be. I really did not need to be reminded of what a stink-fest that day had been.

I swallowed. "I need a real answer," I said. "Did you see someone take my notebook or not?"

"Not exactly," he said. "I didn't see somebody take it. But that's because the person who took it is me."

The answer came so quickly that I didn't know what to say next. I didn't know what I'd been expecting, but definitely not an immediate confession. If Clue were ever on one of those crime TV shows Dad watched all the time from his chair, it'd be the shortest episode in the world.

I cleared my throat. "Okay. That's . . . interesting. Why?"

"Well, I know you write about Zoe all the time."

I frowned. I hated that he knew this.

"And I wanted to borrow it for a little bit. It's for an important experiment I'm doing that's related."

My eyes narrowed. "An experiment that's related?" I asked him. "What does that even mean? And even if it means something that I would be okay with, have you not heard of *asking* before you just take somebody's stuff?"

Clue looked at his feet. "I'm sorry," he mumbled. "I just wanted to . . . I don't know. Can you just trust me?"

I peered up at the big clock in the front of the room. We only had a minute before the bell rang and we'd both be forced out into the super-crowded hall where it'd be impossible to find a place to finish our talk.

Clue looked at the clock too.

"Can you just tell me more about what you're doing? Or better yet, give my notebook back, Clue? It's pretty personal."

"Not yet," he said. "I'm sorry. I just need a little time."

I sucked in my cheeks as more words spilled out. "But it doesn't matter if you need more time. It's mine and I want it back."

"What if I told you that I was using it to give you a big surprise?"

I folded my arms over my chest. "What kind of surprise?"

His mouth curled into a smile. "If I told you, then it wouldn't be a surprise anymore."

The bell rang, and I froze as everyone around me scattered. How could he do this? *How?* Did he know how much I needed Zoe? And as bad as it was for me to be without her, it would be worse for Dad. How was I going to read Dad today's story when today's story—and all the other stories—were in someone else's hands? I tried to swallow the huge lump in my throat, but it wouldn't budge. In fact, the more I tried to gulp it down, the bigger it got.

I wanted to yell at Clue, to shake him, to shout, "Don't you realize how important this is?" But all that came out was a whisper. "Please?"

If he didn't give it back now, he probably wouldn't return it later today, either. And then it'd be the weekend and I'd have no chance of getting Zoe back until Monday, which might as well have been ten thousand million years away.

He edged toward the door as the bell rang. "I'm going to take good care of your notebook. I promise. And if it works, which it should, the surprise will blow your mind."

But I didn't want a surprise that would blow my mind, or any surprise. I just wanted Zoe.

≈

The rest of the day went by in a blur. Whatever I ate for lunch didn't taste like anything, whatever people were talking about I didn't hear, and I had no idea what happened in the rest of my classes. I barely even heard Mrs. Yang when she asked, "Word count?" after lunch.

I barely even said, "Zero," before I teared up and walked away.

I probably could have told Mrs. Yang. She probably could have gotten my notebook back for me. But wasn't I a little old to tattle, even if I was in the middle of a mega crisis? It was like Mom said: *If you have any problems that you think you might be able to work out on your own, well, it'd be really helpful if you tried.*

Obviously Mom and Dad still wanted me to deal with things on my own. That hadn't changed since fourth grade. And it seemed like in sixth grade, most teachers wanted you to figure things out yourself too. Even the really nice ones who asked you how many words you'd written at lunch and whether you had any cool new Oppservations.

After school Bo and I walked home and went into the den, where Dad sat in his chair in front of the TV as usual. His whole face lit up when he saw us, but instead of making me feel better, it made the lump in my throat feel like it had grown to the size of a balloon. A hot air balloon, that was. The kind that could fit our entire family, plus twelve thousand of our closest friends. How was I going to tell him my notebook was gone? Dad counted on hearing my stories after school, the same way I counted on things like eating and sleeping and breathing.

"There are my . . . two . . . favorite kids," he said. His voice went up at the end like a question. He peered at my empty arms. "Zoe taking a nap?" he asked.

When I didn't answer, he added, "Hey, why the long face? Is it me? I know I'm having a bad no-hair day, but there's no need to look so sad about it."

I tried to smile but it was no use. My face was all, *Thanks for the offer, but I'd rather stay worried.*

After Bo told him a story about his day, Dad's eyes turned to me. "So? What's going on, Jadey? How's Zoe today?"

I twisted my hands together. They were very sweaty all of a sudden.

"She's . . . um . . . yeah."

Well, that didn't come out so great.

I had to decide what to do, fast. Mom and Dad would worry if they knew what happened today, and worrying could land Dad right back in the hospital. Mom had basically told me so herself when she told me to deal with my problems without them. I had to be tough.

"I wrote a scene where we sang and danced in my room last night," I finally said. I didn't mention that today in school she got kidnapped.

Dad raised the spots on his face where his eyebrows should have been. His head-hairs weren't the only ones that were missing.

"Did this impromptu musical happen during homework time, by any chance?"

I made a face. "I got it done, don't worry. And I made sure Zoe got hers done too."

"It's a good thing she's got you to take care of her." He squeezed my arm. "What's on the agenda for the weekend?" Dad closed his eyes. Sometimes he liked to imagine my stories like movies in his head. He had seen all the real movies already, he told me. And anyway, mine were much better than anything he could find on our eight channels. Including the crime shows.

I wanted to tell him we were living in a real-life crime show now. I wanted to tell him about Clue stealing my notebook so bad it hurt, but I couldn't.

The idea of Clue reading my stories made me too anxious to even mention anything about it. I'd just have to figure it out myself, like I'd been trying to do whenever any problem came along.

I'd figure. It. Out.

And until that happened, I'd lie.

"We have some super fun stuff planned this weekend," I said. I tried to imagine what I would write about if I still had my notebook. I could write on something else, sure, but it wouldn't be the same. Mrs. Yang always said that looking at your old work could give you ideas for new stuff. If I couldn't write in my notebook, I didn't want to write at all.

"We might go for a walk," I said, "or make some funny videos to put online, or try to bake something, maybe."

"Not banana bread, I hope."

I groaned. Dad really needed to let that go. Mom had this amazing banana bread recipe that used two full bags of chocolate chips, and once, last year, I wrote a story where Zoe and I decided to make it ourselves. We got a teeny bit distracted while it was in the oven, though, and before we even knew what was happening, the smoke alarm was blaring, and firefighters were practically knocking down my door.

It was not our most successful hangout. Of course, it hadn't happened in real life or anything, but it still felt real to me. And to Dad.

"Not banana bread," I agreed.

"Good." Dad smiled, his eyes still closed. "I hope Zoe won't be too disappointed. I know that's her favorite."

"She won't be," I said. "She'll be okay."

Dad pulled me close to him again and kissed the top of my head.

"We all will," he said. And for that one second, I let myself believe him.

7

The Forbidden Pond

The I-miss-Zoe funny feeling didn't go away that night or even the next one. I tried to write on some loose paper I found near Bo's side of our room, but something about it didn't feel right. Zoe wasn't really gone unless I stopped writing about her, but it was like her whole life, our whole entire history, had completely evaporated into thin air.

On the outside, I smiled at Dad's goofy jokes and thanked Mom for the awesome dinner she made Friday night and the yummy breakfast on Saturday morning. But on the inside I felt like I could burst into tears at any second. All Mom had to do was say we were having poached eggs (gross) instead of scrambled (yum) and I'd be done for. I almost wished something like that happened; that way I could get my tears out and blame it on something silly, the kind of thing that would make Mom raise her eyebrows at Dad like, *Our kid is losing it over eggs. Oh, well, she'll get over it soon,* and not like, *Oh, it turns out our daughter's special notebook is missing; this is a very serious problem we will probably want to help her solve even though we are super tired and stressed out and she should be able to deal with it herself.*

Sleeping was pretty much impossible. Both Friday and Saturday night, I lay there forever, tossing and turning, missing my not-so-imaginary friend, and listening to Bo's noisy breathing. He was so lucky he was five and had no idea what was going on with Dad. It was normal to him to always see Dad sitting in that chair and wearing different hats. He probably didn't even remember that first day at the hospital. All Bo had to worry about was playing and drawing, and he didn't have any problems there.

Sunday crawled by the way commercials do when you're watching your favorite show. That's how the whole weekend felt—like one big, long, never-ending commercial. I needed to get back to school. I needed to get my notebook. I needed to rescue Zoe.

But I couldn't, not yet. All I could do was wait.

Only waiting was really boring. So I came up with something else.

"Can I go for a walk?" I asked Mom. "Just around the block or something. Not far."

Bo appeared out of nowhere. "Can I come too?" he asked. He waved a piece of paper in the air. "A long time ago I made a picture of Jade defeating the bad guy outside and so I can bring it if he comes and she needs help."

Mom and I looked at each other and tried not to giggle. Bo was an abstract artist, and it wasn't always clear what his pictures were actually supposed to be. Most of them involved someone or something defeating the bad guy. The bad guys always looked the same—big gray cylinders wearing crowns and angry faces. No one knew why Bo made them with crowns on their heads. He never gave us the reason, and I'd stopped asking. It was just Bo.

"I was actually hoping I could go by myself," I said. I ruffled Bo's fluffy brown hair. "Nothing personal." If I couldn't be with Zoe, I didn't really want to be with anyone else.

Mom turned to Bo. "Want to help me do some painting?" she asked.

"I do," he shouted. He scurried upstairs, probably to get his smock, all thoughts of a walk with me totally forgotten.

"Don't be gone too long," Mom told me.

"Okay."

There was a weird pang in my side as I closed the door to the sounds of Mom and Bo giggling together. I wondered what they were going to paint. I wondered how they could be so happy when Dad was in the next room, barely handling his last round of chemo. I wondered why my whole body felt weak when, for a few seconds, I hadn't even been thinking about the fact that Zoe was gone.

I swallowed hard and took a few steps toward James and Charlie's house across the street. Those bunnies were all over that yard so much it was only right to give them names. The dead grass must taste like bunny food or something, because James and Charlie sat there like they owned the place. And maybe they did. There'd been a *sold* sign on that house forever, but no sign of actual people. That wasn't unusual, though. Our street had a lot of empty houses. All the streets did.

I passed more houses. Most of them had fences around them and plastic toys in the yard. There were a bunch of little kids playing outside the yellow one on the corner, but the streets were mostly quiet.

I rounded the corner and eyed the gravelly path to my right. The path led to the small woodsy area that surrounded Tiveda Pond. I'd only been there once, right after I started writing about Zoe. I thought it'd be a great setting for a story, and it was. Except when Mom found out I'd gone there, she said I shouldn't go there again because nobody really took care of the pond or went there. It was too far off the beaten path, she'd always say.

So, yeah, technically I knew I wasn't supposed to go to the pond. But there was literally nowhere else exciting to walk to in this town, and I had nothing fun to do. So I glanced down the gravel path again. I looked left and right, took a big breath, and walked toward it.

Just like I thought it would be, the area around the pond was empty. Mom was right—the pond looked like it could use a little love. I definitely didn't remember its greenish glow and slimy-looking bubbles from the last time I went. A cloudy mist hovered directly above it. I considered keeping an eye out for a witch, because the water totally looked like some kind of potion.

A plopping sound echoed through the air, making me jump. I looked back toward the water and blinked a few thousand times to make sure I was seeing right. Clue was *in the pond*—just his feet and shins, but still, *in it*—wading around like he was in a sparkly blue swimming pool, not goop-infested water that was probably going to give him a disease or turn him into a sea creature.

My jaw dropped as I tried to figure out what to do. While I was thinking, Clue climbed out of the water. He held a long tube in one hand. It was filled to the top with gross green liquid. As I watched, he grabbed a backpack from the ground and pulled something out. My notebook! Was he going to . . . he wouldn't . . . would he? I tried to charge out there, but my feet refused to move, so I held my breath and braced myself for the worst. Clue tipped the tube toward my notebook . . . and let *one, two, three* single drops fall onto the cover.

What was he *doing*?

Clue tucked my notebook back inside his bag as if nothing weird had happened. He pulled out another notebook—the green one I'd seen him writing in at school sometimes—and jotted something down. Even from a little distance away, I could see the look on his face. It was an oppservation face. Excited looking, but also sad enough to smash your heart to pieces.

My heart raced. If I was going to say something, I had to do it now. "Clue!" I called out.

When he saw me, his face turned to pure panic. He grabbed his bag and stumbled over grass and twigs as he ran away in the opposite direction.

Just like that, I was alone again at the pond.

I watched the water, which felt like the weirdest thing ever. At least I knew that Clue hadn't ripped my notebook to shreds and thrown it in the pond. He still had it. It would be hard, but I could survive one more night and get it back tomorrow.

Slowly I turned toward the gravel path and made my way home. The pond seemed to bubble gently as I walked away.

8
A New Neighbor

I knew Mom told me not to be gone long. And even though it was probably getting close to long, I wandered back home slowly, stopping to watch cars drive back and forth, kick some loose pebbles, and think. What I had seen didn't seem real, but it was. It happened so fast that maybe I imagined it or saw it wrong. But it kept replaying in my mind. It was more confusing than anything I could ever come up with, and I was a writer. It *had* happened.

I stopped when I came to my front yard. I hadn't really noticed my yard lately, or thought about it, because who really thinks about their yard? From this spot, it was impossible *not* to notice. Even though Tiveda in general was kind of brown and dead, our yard was different. Well, not now. But in the past. Before Dad got sick, we had bright green grass, colorful flowers, even one of those little decorative gnome-y guys with the beard and the pointy red hat. Now the grass was brown, the flowers were dead, and the gnome's chipping paint made it look like a zombie. Even on a sunny day, the outside of our house looked almost as gloomy as the inside felt.

I sighed and opened the door.

"Hello?"

No answer.

I wandered through the den where Dad was sleeping in his chair and made my way into the kitchen. There was a note on the fridge. *Went to grab ice cream at the gas station. Back soon. Love, Mom and Bo.* Next to the words, there was a picture of an ice cream cone poking Bo's bad guy with a sprinkle.

I went back to the den, sat on the couch across from Dad, and stared blankly out the window. A few loud beeps jerked my attention to the house across the street. It looked like the bunnies were finally getting some company.

A big truck backed into the driveway, and once

it came to a stop, a girl leapt out looking especially happy. It was like she hadn't seen the sun in a thousand years. Her long dark hair flew behind her as she skipped in circles around the driveway before collapsing on the lawn. She didn't seem to mind at all that the grass was as brown as ours.

I knew I should get up and go turn on the TV or something. It didn't matter who this girl was. Even though she looked like she could maybe be my age or close to it, and even if it turned out she was in sixth grade and was fun to be around, it didn't matter. She'd be gone soon enough, like most people in this town. Anyway, my notebook was the only real friend I needed. Once I got that back tomorrow, I'd be fine.

But still. This girl was kind of interesting. After she got up from the grass, she stood in front of the house and stared at it for what felt like hours. Then she turned around and smiled at our street like it was the most amazing thing she'd ever seen in her life. I ducked so she couldn't see me watching her. But she wasn't even looking my way. She was looking at the world like she was so incredibly happy to see it, even though it was home to brown grass and dead flowers and zombie gnomes.

I sat up a teeny bit straighter. Our street was pretty narrow, so the girl was actually not that far away from me. I could make out some of the details of her face: she had bright, sparkly green eyes and this funny-shaped blob on her face, right above her eyebrow, which was probably some sort of birth-mark.

As I looked closer, I noticed that it *was* a birth-mark—and it almost looked heart-shaped, like Zoe's.

I frowned to myself. I was going so bonkers without my notebook that I was seeing Zoe's features in this new neighbor girl. While I was at it, maybe later I'd see Zoe's face reflected in the mirror or in a piece of fruit.

I kept watching. I kind of couldn't look away.

And what I saw next was freakier than fruit with a face.

The girl ran to the mailbox at the edge of her driveway and pulled three big red stickers out of her jeans pocket. She stuck them on the mailbox and then stood back to admire her work.

I practically fell off the couch.

The stickers on the mailbox spelled Z-O-E.

At that moment Dad made a super loud snoring sound, which almost made me fall off the couch again. He opened his eyes, blinked a few times, and stretched.

I looked back out the window. The girl was gone. But the letters on the mailbox were still there, and the image of her face was front and center in my mind.

It probably wasn't possible. No, forget the probably. It *wasn't* possible. Maybe it was her last name. It'd be an unusual one, sure, but I wasn't going to judge.

Dad rubbed his forehead. "I think I had a weird dream," he told me.

I took a long breath in and out. I hadn't been asleep, but still.

"I think I did too," I said.

9

The New Girl's First Day

When my alarm went off on Monday morning, I practically leapt out of bed. I had never been so excited to get out of bed on a Monday or maybe ever. Today was the day I would get my notebook back from Clue. Plus, maybe I would meet the girl from across the street.

I'd tossed and turned all night thinking about her and about what I'd seen at the pond. Just because she looked like Zoe and lived across the street like Zoe and, oh, yeah, might actually be *named* Zoe, didn't necessarily mean anything. And as for Clue, maybe he was a budding marine biologist or something. Didn't they like to study weird water? I just hoped he wasn't planning to surprise me by writing over all my stories with bizarre pond-water observations.

I looked for the girl across the street and Clue all morning, but I didn't see them until third-period science. I was gearing up to tell Clue that I was ready for my notebook back, but then there she was, standing in the corner at the front of the room. Usually people were noisy until class started, but it was weirdly quiet. Everybody's eyes were on the new girl.

"I'm sure you've noticed that Holland and Eva are no longer with us," Mrs. Wilson said. "Their families have relocated. It's disappointing, but I know they'll stay in touch and come visit us soon."

The teachers said that every time, but by now, we knew it wasn't true.

"I do have some good news, though," Mrs. Wilson continued, pointing at the new girl, who smiled. "We've got a new student joining us today. I'd like to introduce you all to Zoe."

Zoe.

Her first name.

I could *not* believe it.

Mrs. Wilson turned to her. "I'm sure everyone will make you feel welcome. Go ahead and take whichever open seat you'd like."

Everyone's faces said, *Pick me! Let me be your Tiveda best friend! I'm the one you want!*

But Zoe wasn't looking at any of them.

Because she was looking right at *me*.

And maybe I was imagining it, but she was almost looking at me like I was the only one in the room. The only one in the world, even. It was like she was telling me We Are Going to Be Best Friends Forever and Ever No Matter What.

I bit the inside of my lip and watched her right back. Everything that was happening was creepily similar to what had happened in my very first Zoe story. But before I could think about that any more, Zoe slid into the open seat on my left.

My jaw dropped. No. Way. I scanned the room. There was one open seat (Eva's old spot) by the window. And there was Holland's old spot—one of the only desks in the whole school that had that little bar underneath where you could put your feet. Those two seats were pretty much the best you could get.

But as luck would have it, Zoe hadn't chosen either of the good seats. She'd chosen a regular old,

nothing-special desk near the middle of the room. Right next to me.

Mrs. Wilson started talking about some science-y thing, but I couldn't concentrate on a word she said. Because as I looked over at Zoe, she pulled out two pencils from her pocket and placed them on her desk.

And they weren't any old pencils.

They were blue. And sparkly. Just like mine.

This was getting seriously weird. I was obviously losing my mind from not getting enough sleep this weekend. Right after class I'd go splash cold water in my face, and then I'd get down to business and force Clue to give me my notebook. I'd quit panicking, and I'd look at the new girl more closely and realize that she was a completely different Zoe than my Zoe. And then I'd go home and sleep forever. I wouldn't even watch whatever random thing I found on TV or online. Only bed. Sleep, sleep, and more sleep.

It was an excellent plan, so why wouldn't my heart stop pounding a gazillion miles a minute?

I turned to Zoe, who was looking at my pencils.

She giggled. And even though things were more freaky than funny right now, I couldn't help myself—I did too. A lot.

We giggled so much that Mrs. Wilson stopped mid-sentence and said, "Jade, Zoe, would you please go out into the hall and calm yourselves down?"

I had never been in trouble before. But for some reason, it didn't feel that bad.

Once we left the classroom, I took a big, deep, larger-than-life breath. This was my chance to figure out what was going on. All signs pointed to this Zoe being my Zoe, but things like that didn't happen in real life. My Zoe was a made-up character. This Zoe was a human being. They were pretty different things.

Weren't they?

"I'm Zoe, by the way."

Her voice made me jump. It sounded as bright as her eyes. (Not that a voice could really be bright like an eye. But it was, somehow.) Everything about her screamed happy and fun and bold and strong.

She was a pop song.

And I was freaking. Out.

"I know," I said. My voice shook a little, the same way it did when I'd read my first Zoe story to Dad. "The teacher just introduced you. I'm Jade."

"I know," she said.

"How?"

I knew how. What I didn't know was why the word had popped out of my mouth automatically.

"Because you just told me," Zoe answered. Then she started giggling again. And I didn't know why, or how, or anything, pretty much—but I started up again too. And we didn't stop for a long, long time. Even though I still didn't get what was going on, the feeling that filled me up as I sat there with Zoe was the best one I'd had in a very long time.

≈

I had no idea what we did during the rest of class, once Zoe and I finally went back in.

But what I did know was that the second the bell rang, I tapped Clue on the shoulder.

"I know you know that I saw you *and my notebook* at the pond yesterday," I told him. "It seems like you're done doing whatever you were doing, so maybe I can have it back now? I think I've been really patient."

"Do you like your surprise?" he asked.

"Huh?"

He smiled as we edged toward the hallway. "I did it," he said slowly, like he couldn't really believe it himself. "I really did it." I didn't know exactly what an eye twinkle looked like, but I was pretty confident that I was seeing one on Clue's face right now.

"She was right," he said. "I can't believe I waited this long to try." Now it seemed like he was talking more to himself than to me. "She always had these big theories. Raindrops shaped like hearts know the future. If you make a wish from the top of a mountain, it'll come true." He laughed. "We'd go play by the pond, and she'd say that the water was made of magic. That maybe it held all the secrets of this town. That one day, maybe it would be able to make the secrets come to life. It always sounded so silly. But she was right, Jade. She was right."

"*She?*" I could barely follow his rant.

"My sister, Harper." He paused. "Never mind."

"Your sister thinks the pond is magical? It knows secrets? Clue, what the heck are you talking about?"

The questions spilled out of my mouth like the little drops from our leaky kitchen sink Dad hadn't gotten around to fixing. Nothing he was saying made sense.

"Zoe's real," he said. "Your secret is alive," he said. "And soon, mine will be too." He held out my notebook. "Thanks for letting me borrow it. And just so you know, I didn't read a thing."

The hairs on my arms stood up.

I forgot about all my questions for a second as I lunged for the notebook. I clutched it tightly in my arms. There it was, my yellow cover, filled pages and all. You couldn't even tell it'd gotten wet.

I looked Clue in the eye and tried to wrap my mind around all the things he'd just said. Did he really bring Zoe to life? But that was impossible. There was no way. Except . . . Mrs. Yang says writers make impossible things real all the time. Maybe other people could too. With help from magical, secret-knowing ponds.

"You really did it?" I asked.

He nodded slowly. "I really did. Well, with some help."

I still couldn't quite believe it. But Mrs. Yang said that sometimes you didn't need to write every detail about how every little thing worked, or even know those details as a reader. You just needed to go with it. To sit back, relax, and enjoy the story.

I didn't know if I'd be able to do much relaxing, but if Zoe had really come to life . . . well, *that* I could definitely enjoy.

"So . . . what now?" I asked.

He shrugged.

"Now, have fun. And maybe write some more," he called as he walked away, "so we can see what happens next."

I had to get to Mrs. Yang's class, but my feet wouldn't budge. Instead I just kind of stood there with my mouth hanging open as people swerved around me like I was one of the random poles in the hall. Everyone and everything looked blurry. I had so many questions. I tried to think, but my brain was too full and too empty at the same time.

It was real, though. It was really real. Clue did something with my notebook and the water from the pond, and somehow, Zoe had come to life.

A grin spread across my face. *It was real.*

A hand grabbed my shoulder and gently steered me to the side of the hall.

"Where are you going, Jade?" Mrs. Yang asked with a chuckle. "Our class is right here. You seem in better spirits than you were last Friday after lunch. Is everything okay now?"

"Oh, everything's okay," I told her. "Everything is more than okay."

I thought about the notebook still safely in my hands, and Clue's words. *Write more.* He made a good point. Zoe seemed to know my old stories already (the very first ones, at least) so maybe I should give her—give *us*—some new material. She did exactly what I'd written before, from moving into the house across the street to breaking out those two sparkly blue pencils. But if I wrote something new, would she do that too?

I smiled at Mrs. Yang. "I'm going to go sit down," I told her. I grinned at my notebook. "I have to get writing."

10
The Best Time Ever

I looked at the blank page in front of me and felt more inspired than ever. Energy zipped up and down my spine. These words I was about to write were more important than anything I'd ever written before.

Zoe had seriously no idea how she got to Tiveda Middle, but she didn't really care—she was just excited to be there. She could tell that Jade was going to be her best friend ever in the entire world, and they were going to have a ton of fun together.

At the same time, a part of her was scared. She got a weird flippy-floppy feeling in her stomach. It felt like she was on a roller coaster with no end in sight.

"Are you okay?" Mrs. Yang's soft voice interrupted my thoughts. I looked up and scanned the room. Then I saw Zoe. She sat hunched over in her chair, holding her stomach.

Zoe holding her stomach like that, that couldn't have been because . . . was that . . . did I *do* that?

I stared at my paper. If I did that, not only did new Zoe stories happen in real life—they happened *fast*.

She mumbled a yes to Mrs. Yang, but it sounded fake.

Zoe felt better, I wrote.

She smiled and sat up straight. "Yup, I'm okay. All good."

And it really seemed like she was.

Whoa.

I tapped my eraser to my chin. There was still a chance that that was just a coincidence. I had to get creative—write something so wacky that it couldn't be normal if it happened. If something especially bizarre happened, I'd know *for sure* it was because I'd written it. But it also had to be something that wouldn't totally freak out Mrs. Yang or get anyone in major trouble.

Zoe decided to sing "Twinkle, Twinkle, Little Star."

I put my pencil down. If this was really Zoe, she'd totally be up for a little song. She loved to sing and dance.

I twisted my hands together. They were super, super sweaty. This was it. This was how I'd know for sure.

As if in slow motion, Zoe got to her feet. She opened her mouth.

And she sang the song.

Every. Last. Word.

You couldn't hear a single sound in the whole room, not even a whisper. Even Mrs. Yang was speechless, and she always knew what to say. Finally Clue smacked his hands together and clapped, and everyone joined in, even the Sparkle Girls who wore a lot of sparkles and seemed like they're kind of hard to impress.

I glanced at Clue. He raised his eyebrows.

She actually sang the song. She *sang the song!* How . . . what? Nobody randomly sang "Twinkle, Twinkle, Little Star" at the beginning of English class. Or any class. Not even music class, usually. And I couldn't forget the whole sparkly pencil meeting-each-other thing earlier and the moving-in thing from over the weekend. There was only one explanation: the stories from my notebook were coming true. And the new things I wrote were coming true too.

Whatever Clue did—it really worked. I guess the weird pond water wasn't just weird. Like he said, somehow . . . it was magical too.

"Okay, Zoe," said Mrs. Yang. She motioned to everybody like it was time to stop clapping. "Thank you for that. Let's move on now."

Zoe smiled, and Mrs. Yang continued her lesson.

≈

I really wanted to talk to Clue after class, but not as much as I wanted and needed to talk to Zoe. The Sparkles got to her first, though. I could hear them squealing about her "Twinkle, Twinkle" performance from across the room. I couldn't really blame them for being excited. She was the coolest person ever, after all, and it had been pretty epic. One of those things people would talk about for years to come, probably.

Anyway, once we got to lunch, she'd forget all about them. I just knew it.

And I was right.

When I got to the cafeteria, I saw her sitting all by herself at the table where I did my writing every day. She was waiting for me. She had to be. My heart flip-flopped a thousand times over. It was like the time back in Nevada when I'd begged Mom and Dad to drive me to the kid's bookstore an hour away to meet my favorite author. We waited in line for what felt like years. But when we finally got to the front, everything about the day that had been boring or annoying or made me impatient totally disappeared. The author smiled at me, and I knew that the trip was worth it. Hanging out with Zoe would be even better. She was my best friend, sure, but she was also kind of like a celebrity I'd been obsessed with basically forever.

I took a few steps forward, but then I paused.

And without my permission, my feet took one giant step back.

What was *that* about?

I tried again. Two steps forward. One step back. And again.

It was like I was dancing. With myself. And not very well.

There was no reason to be nervous, but maybe my feet were trying to tell me that I was. I tucked a loose piece of hair behind my ear. When had my ear gotten so hot? I felt my cheeks, my forehead, my chin. Everything was hot. And scrunchy, too, like my face was trying to figure out an answer to a teacher's question without any help from Clue.

I swallowed hard. I'd probably been nervous hanging out with my favorite author too. But now, years later, I only remembered that exciting, amazing feeling of seeing her smile at me when I got to the front of the line.

With that in the very front of my brain, I finally rushed over to Zoe and sat down before I could change my mind, or my feet could change it for me.

"Hi," I said. And then I grinned. I was okay. It was my best friend! Here! In front of me! It was like my birthday and Hanukkah and New Year's all rolled into one incredible moment of amazingness.

"This might sound weird," she said, leaning in, "but I had this feeling that I was supposed to sit here. Like my feet came right to this table all on their own."

"Well, we're sort of best friends," I told her. "I mean, we are best friends, and we sit here every day. This might sound weird, but I write these stories about this girl named Zoe—you. And in the stories, we do a ton of fun stuff together."

"I'm Zoe," she said, like she was introducing herself all over again.

"Yeah, I know. You're Zoe, the character from my stories. I made you up. You lived in a notebook, I guess. But Clue brought you to life."

"What's a clue?" Zoe picked something up off her lunch tray. "And what's this?"

I giggled. "That's a spork," I said. Then I pointed at the table a couple rows over where Clue sat with a few guys from our English class. "And that's Clue."

"Spork," Zoe repeated. "Clue!"

"Very good," I said.

She stuck her tongue out at me, but in a joking kind of way.

I tilted my head to the side as Zoe admired her spork some more. It was pretty funny that she'd never heard of one. Around here they were as common as new mailmen. But maybe it wasn't funny at all. I tried to think if I'd ever written about a spork in a Zoe story. If I had, maybe she'd know what they were. But if I hadn't . . . she might not have a clue.

If that was the case, what else did she know? And what else *didn't* she know?

I held up my napkin. "Do you know what this is?" I asked.

"Napkin," she answered. "But works better as a bird."

Whoa. I smiled and pointed to a milk carton. "How about this?"

"Milk carton."

"Nice."

I pointed to a grape. "This?"

Zoe frowned and tilted her head so far to the side that she had to blow hair out of her face.

"A . . . something something?"

"Close. It's actually called a grape."

"Oh," she said. "Interesting. *Grape. Grape grape grape.*"

Apparently I needed to write more stories that involved fruit. That made me wonder something else. I leaned in. "Do you know our stories?" I asked. "Like everything we've done together?"

"Everything around here seems familiar, but fuzzy, you know? It's like I've seen everything before, but through blurry glasses or something. All I know for sure is I was in this moving thing, and then I was in a house, and now I'm here," Zoe said. "I don't re-member much before that." She tapped her fingers on her chin like she was thinking. "I'm alive," she said, but it came out more like a question.

"You are," I said. I smiled. So she didn't know the details of our adventures—that was okay. She had the general knowledge of things that were in them, like origami napkins and milk mustaches and stuff. We'd bring the stories to life together, the way we'd made some of them come true already.

Zoe grinned from ear to ear.

"Best friends," she said.

"Best friends," I agreed.

Zoe did a little dance in her seat. "We're going to have the best time ever."

I smiled, leaned in as much as my seat would allow, and lightly grabbed her wrists. I'm not sure why or what I was even trying to do.

The weird thing was, I wrote a story last year where this happened at lunch. First I grabbed her wrists. Then she wriggled out of my grasp, flipped her wrists over so she was actually grabbing mine, and before I knew it we were playing that fun hand-slappy game where you try to catch the other person before they pull away.

Now that was exactly what was happening. And as fun as it had been in my imagination, the real thing was about a trillion times better. It was so awesome that my old stories were actually happening, and that new things I wrote were coming true too.

Zoe and I laughed really hard and really loud

and it might have been too loud but I didn't care. I could feel tons of best-friend duos looking at us, probably sighing and wishing that they were having this much fun.

Zoe was right. We totally would have the best time ever.

We already were.

"So catch me up," she said, after we were done with our game.

"On what?"

"Us. Our stories. Grapes. Everything I've missed."

"Oh, right." I grinned. "Yeah, I'll catch you up."

For the rest of lunch, that's just what I did.

11
Liver Alone

*L*unch flew by faster than it ever had in the history of lunch. When the bell rang I refused to move until it rang a second time so I could make sure that it wasn't an accident. We'd just sat down! How could it be time to go already? But it was, so Zoe and I got up and walked toward the classrooms with everybody else. It didn't feel like there were sixtyish sixth graders shuffling down the hall with us, though. There was only us. Zoe and Jade. Jade and Zoe. Best friends.

"Word count?" Ms. Yang asked as we passed her by.

"Zero!" I shouted.

Maybe she said something else after that, but I

didn't hear. I had one earbud in and Zoe had the other, and we were singing along like every song was recorded just for us.

I skipped into fifth-period health with her by my side. Normally health grossed me out before it even started, but nothing could bug me today. I felt like I could survive forty-five minutes of the digestive system and anything else that Mr. Kremen threw our way. Except for maybe the scary-looking bowl on his desk that was filled with what looked like a combination of dog food and puke.

He grinned at it and then at all of us.

"Isn't this unit the greatest?" he asked. "Soak it up, people, because soon we are on to mental, emotional, and social health. All good things, of course. But today, our exciting tour of the digestive system continues with the one, the only, the liver!"

Some people giggled, but not me. There was nothing funny about a liver. Especially the ones that stopped working.

As if he could read my mind, Mr. Kremen shot me a look—but since he was the teacher and everybody was watching him, it was kind of like he was shooting the whole class the look that was only meant for me, which was not so great. His face was part sad and part worried. Even his pointy gray hairs seemed to stare at me that same way.

He opened his mouth. *Don't say anything out loud,* I begged inside my head. But if he had read my mind before, he definitely wasn't doing it now.

"Jade, if you're uncomfortable at any point, feel free to leave," he said. "You don't have to ask first or anything. Or, if there's anything you want to add to our discussion, you can do that too. You probably know more than I do. However you want to participate or not participate—it's up to you."

I squirmed around in my seat. My cheeks burned. Mr. Kremen was probably trying to be nice, because my mom told all my teachers that my dad had liver cancer. But did he have to try to be nice in front of the whole class? Now everybody was looking at me. Not even just looking. They were staring, like I had green stuff in my teeth or worse. I shrunk down and tried to make myself as small as I could, but it was no use. Everyone kept right on looking. What did they want me to say? What was I supposed to say?

Wait a second. Maybe I didn't have to say anything out loud. Maybe I could say something on paper, instead, and someone else could be the one to speak.

I hurried to write in my notebook.

Zoe distracted Mr. Kremen and saved the day.

It was kind of a short story, but it got the point across.

"Hey, Mr. K.?"

Zoe's hand shot up and—to my total amazement—everybody's heads turned away from me and toward her.

"What's that stuff on your desk?" she asked.

"Chopped liver," he said. "It's a spread made with eggs, onion, garlic, and chicken liver. Doesn't have much to do with human livers, but I thought we'd stick to a theme today."

"Can I try some?"

Gasps and whispers rippled through the room. I took a giant breath and looked around. Not one person was looking at me. All eyes were on Zoe, just like I wanted.

"I don't know. It was really only here for dramatic effect," Mr. Kremen said. "Though technically it is a food. And personally, I find it very tasty."

"Let her have some!" someone called out. Soon everybody was cheering.

"Okay, okay, quiet down." Mr. Kremen rummaged around in his desk drawer and pulled out a plastic spork like the ones we used at lunch. "If you really want to, go ahead. But if she doesn't want to," he turned toward the class, "you should *liver* alone." He laughed to himself as we all rolled our eyes. He then added, "Is this okay with you, Jade?"

Ugh, not again. I closed my eyes and wished that I were invisible.

"I'm doing it."

I opened my eyes in time to see Zoe spring up from her seat and race to the front of the room. People didn't even have a chance to look at me because she got up there so fast. She dipped the spork into the chopped liver of disgustingness and then held it up and raised her eyebrows at the class like, *Dare me? Double dare me? Triple dare me?*

She put the spork down—but in a joking way— and the whole class booed.

"Just kidding, you guys. I am all about this spork." She picked it up again, smiled, and slipped a giant bite into her mouth.

The room went dead silent as she chewed. People leaned as far forward as their seats would let them, watching like they'd never seen anyone eat anything gross before. Bo used to eat glue like once a week, even after Dad tried to hide it from him. We finally had to come up with a really detailed story about this other three-year-old boy who ate so much glue that he turned into a human glue stick, and not in a fun way. In a very bad, you're-going-to-stick-to-things-that-aren't-very-fun-to-be-stuck-to kind of way. Dad and I acted it out for Bo so he'd understand. I was Regular Bo and Dad was Bo the Human Glue Stick, and all afternoon Dad pretended to stick to everything and get really frustrated when he couldn't go where he wanted. Bo got the idea. Though it kind of stunk that Dad actually did turn into the Human Glue Stick, always stuck to that same brown chair.

Everybody stood and cheered for Zoe as she swallowed. Not a single person glanced my way—not even Mr. Kremen. I grinned for the first time in health class maybe ever. It worked. It had really worked! Together, there was nothing we couldn't do.

≋

OPPSERVATION: It's weird how people always say "think before you speak" but never "think before you listen."

Questions for further research: Shouldn't you try to think no matter what?

Teachers and parents always tell us that we're in

control of what we say. We can think before we speak. But no one ever says you're in control of what you listen to. Sometimes you are, maybe, like with music and TV. But sometimes you have to sit at a hospital and listen to a doctor say things like "liver cancer . . . 50 percent five-year survival rate" that you're not supposed to understand because you're only in fourth grade. But even back then, two whole years ago, I did understand. Even before I started listening to the doctors, I was thinking about how I would never really be ready for anything they were going to say.

Sometimes you have to sit in health class and listen to Mr. Kremen talk about livers. And talk. And talk. And talk.

I knew I could walk out, like he said, but my body felt stuck to my seat. If I got up, everybody would be even more curious than they were before Zoe distracted them. I didn't want to talk about it. I *really* didn't want to be asked about it. I wanted Zoe's spork-fascination and liver-eating to be the most memorable parts of health class. And so I had to stay.

But that didn't mean I had to like it.

I put my elbows on my desk, my head in my hands, and sneakily inched my fingers toward my earrings that looked like owls. Maybe if I could cover even a pinky finger's worth of ear, it would help.

As my pinkies reached their target, Zoe's voice broke through.

"I don't feel very well," she said. Her face was as green as the water in the pond.

"Go to the bathroom," Mr. Kremen said. Now her face was *really* green-ish. "Quickly! And someone go with her."

I jumped up and chased Zoe out the door. Whatever invisible force was holding me in my seat felt like it had suddenly broken. It wasn't good that she felt sick, but this was a great excuse to get out.

The weird thing was, after I was all the way down the hall and into the bathroom and holding Zoe's hair as the chopped liver came back out, I could still hear Mr. Kremen's voice in my head. *Liver alone! Liver! Liver liver liver.*

It was one thing to cover your ears so you wouldn't hear what someone else said out loud. But how could you stop hearing the words in your mind?

"Thanks again." Zoe swished a third gulp of water around in her mouth and spit it out in the bathroom sink. "That was really nice of you to hold my hair."

"It's what best friends do," I said. "Anyway, you helped me too. It was the least I could do."

"Best friends are there for good stuff and bad stuff," she agreed.

"And dumb liver stuff," I said.

"And holding-your-hair-while-you-puke stuff," she added, and we both giggled. "How exactly did I help you?"

"Well, you know I used to write about you," I said. "And earlier I discovered that I still can. I mean, obviously I can. But the things I write actually happen. Like when you sang 'Twinkle, Twinkle,' that was because of me."

The words sounded weird coming out of my mouth. They felt pretend. Like I was Bo, telling some story about my made-up, gray, cylindrical bad guy with a crown. But I wasn't. This was real.

I gulped as it really, truly, deeply sunk in. *This was real.* Zoe was alive. And when I wrote things about her, they actually came true.

It was cool. No, it was *amazing.* So why was a whole bunch of sweat suddenly clinging to my forehead?

Zoe's eyes got huge. "That's so awesome," she said. "I was wondering why I suddenly sang that song."

I giggled, but it came out strained. "Good," I

said. "I'm glad you thought so. I mean, I knew you'd think so. Oh, and I'm really sorry about the liver. I feel kind of bad. But I didn't make you eat it. I just wrote that you distracted Mr. Kremen from talking about me and that you basically saved the day. The eating thing was all you!"

Zoe pretended to gag. "Obviously I have no idea what I'm doing in this weird world of yours. You should probably be super specific when you write about me."

"Sure thing," I said as I wiped a little sweat off my forehead with a paper towel.

What was I so worried about? I knew Zoe better than I knew anyone. I knew what she'd like and what she wouldn't. Sure, I had a lot of control over her, but as long as I wrote stories about things that made her happy, there was nothing to be nervous about. If Clue really did make this happen, I couldn't be mad at him for all the kinks that would need to be worked out. I mean, Zoe was still standing before me. The Zoe *I* created.

"I'm here for you," I told her. And then I started singing. "Twinkle, twinkle . . ." I shot Zoe a look.

"Little star," she chimed in.

And we sang all the way back to class.

12

The Funny Stuff

hen school got out at three, Zoe and I skipped next door to Tiveda Elementary and picked up Bo. I stood up extra straight as I took his hand in mine. I felt different this afternoon. *Good* different. *Important* different.

The kind of different you feel when you have a best friend who is a living, breathing, perfect human being, who has come with you to pick up your brother, because why wouldn't she?

"We're going to walk home with my friend Zoe," I told Bo. "She just moved in across the street."

"Zoe!" he repeated. "That's the same name as your imaginary friend."

I froze.

"Yeah," I said, "but lots of kids have the same name."

"Not me. I'm the only Bo in my whole class."

"Well, you're special. Now come on."

"Can you hold my other hand, Zoe?" Bo asked.

I laughed, even though a weird surge of something—sadness? Jealousy?—zipped through me. Bo had everything so easy. If he wanted a new friend, he just asked, and *bam*, he had one.

Zoe glanced at me, and I nodded.

Bo asked, "Can you swing me back and forth?"

Zoe glanced at me again, and again, I nodded. This was pretty weird, being in charge of someone else's decisions. But at the same time (Oppservation!), it was also really cool to be needed.

"One, two, three, *swing*!" I shouted. Our hands lurched forward, and so did Bo. His little body flung up, up, up, and he landed in a fit of contagious laughs.

"One, two, three, *swing*!" Zoe shouted, and up he went again.

"This is fun," Bo said.

I smiled at the two of them so hard my cheeks hurt.

"Yeah," I said. "It really is."

Mom and Dad's truck pulled into the driveway a couple minutes after we got home and said goodbye to Zoe. Dad had some follow-up doctor appointment, and he looked sleepy, but that didn't stop him from asking his typical end-of-the-day questions only a second after they'd come inside.

"How was school today?" he asked. "What's new with Zoe? Who defeated the bad guy?"

I thought I'd have more time to figure out what I was going to say, but now it was too late. It was one thing to make up a story on the spot when I didn't want him to worry about my stolen notebook. It was something else completely to skip over the little detail that new Zoe was notebook Zoe—a real person who lived across the street, went to my school, and was even more amazing in real life than she was on paper.

I stood on my tiptoes and stared out the front window as Bo started to talk. Zoe waved to me from her window across the street. As much as I wanted to hang out with her every second of every day for the rest of forever, I had to come up with a plan before I brought her around Mom and Dad. Dad especially. He'd heard every single story about her I'd ever written. He knew exactly who she was and what she looked like. If he knew she was real, Dad would be big-time confused, and who knew what being confused could do to his liver and his body. Sure, he was done with chemo for now, but he was also done with chemo toward the end of fifth grade, only then the cancer came back again. So it turned out that he wasn't really done at all. He had to be done for real this time, though. I *needed* him to be done for real. Which meant, for now, I had to keep Zoe away.

Bo finished describing how the bad guy came for his library teacher but she defeated him, because everybody always defeated that bad, bad cylinder thingy with a crown.

"That's great, Bo," Dad said. He scratched the brim of his tall Cat in the Hat hat. "Jade?"

"Um." The question played over and over in my head. What was new with Zoe? Oh, you know. Not much. She tried chopped liver. Wasn't a big fan.

But I didn't say that. I didn't say anything, because my mouth got way too dry and scratchy to even swallow, let alone make words come out. It felt like a desert in there, cacti and all.

Luckily Mom burst into the living room. Her long hair was up in a messy bun with big strands escaping and going every which way. She brushed a big piece out of her face with a rubber-glove-covered hand. "Has anyone seen the dustbuster?"

"She decided it's cleaning night," Dad told us.

"Hi to you too," I said.

"Sorry," Mom said, and leaned over to kiss both of us on the tops of our heads. "Hi. Love you. Sorry," she repeated. "You know how I get. It's hard to stop. Hi."

"You've barely started," I told her. "But hi."

Mom and Bo were both like that. Besides their hot-fudge colored hair and their love of monster movies, neither one liked to stop once they'd started a project.

Mom jogged in place, like standing was too boring for her so she had to spice it up. "So, dustbuster? Anyone? No? If you were a dustbuster, where would you be?"

"Lego Land," said Bo.

"A bookstore," I said.

"My doctor's office, no contest," said Dad.

We all looked at each other and totally cracked up. My family was so weird. Lego Land. A bookstore. Dad's doctor's office. Yeah, right. We hadn't left Colorado in two years—and we definitely weren't going anywhere anytime soon—so how the heck would our dustbuster go clean any of those places? Except Dad did live at the doctor's. So that one was actually realistic.

OPPSERVATION: My family laughs at things that shouldn't be funny, once you think about it.

Questions for further research: Why doesn't anything ever happen to us that's really funny?

"Okay, new plan," Mom said, flicking some dust off her face. "Dance party."

She tapped something on her phone and soon the whole room was thumping with some funny kid song. Dad clapped his hands as Mom spun Bo and me around. We shouted and squealed and twirled in big circles, our arms waving and our feet flailing. We flew around the room. I closed my eyes, soaking it in. It had been a weird day. But a pretty good one too. Maybe my family could laugh for normal reasons sometimes after all.

≈

After the dance party I raced up to my room and went straight to the window. I should've been tired, but I had more energy than ever. My window faced the same direction as the one in the living room, so

I could still see Zoe sitting by her front window. She waved to me right away with both arms, like she'd been watching my window all night, waiting for me to appear behind it.

I mouthed "what's" and then pointed up at the ceiling.

Zoe pointed up at her ceiling, too, like she was answering, "the ceiling."

The whole thing felt kind of familiar, like it had happened before. As I held up a finger almost automatically, I realized—it had! This was a story I'd written over the summer. We were both bored but we couldn't hang out for some reason, and since neither of us had cell phones, we were stuck watching each other through our windows like people in the olden days. I'd said, "What's up?" and she'd said, "The ceiling," just like this. Now we were going to play charades, which was going to be hilarious because we couldn't actually guess each other's words unless we somehow magically became master lip readers. I'd held up one finger because I was going to act out one word—*monkey*. Next Zoe would hold up two fingers and pretend to be a vampire chicken. (That's what I thought she was, anyway. I never really found out for sure.) This would go on pretty much forever, with little breaks here and there for snacks and hysterical giggling.

We played until it was so dark that we could barely see each other's windows, just like in the story. When the game ended and the world became pitch black, I stayed calm and happy.

Even though I couldn't see her anymore, I knew she was still there. And *alive*.

I fell asleep with a smile on my face.

13
The Window Seat

I practically flew out of bed the next morning, just like I had the day before, but for a slightly different reason. I didn't need to chase Clue down for my notebook, but I did need the fun to start as soon as possible. For the second time this week—and possibly for the second time forever—I didn't want to press the snooze alarm a thousand times and then drag myself through the motions of getting ready for school. I wanted to speed through them—while twirling, maybe—like a famous award-winning author.

School, I thought to myself as I brushed my teeth, washed my face, and got dressed. *School!* With a real best friend. With the *best* best friend.

While I was getting ready, Bo had finished his picture of a lamp defeating the bad guy. We hugged Mom and Dad goodbye, and then we were off.

I grabbed his hand and pulled him up Zoe's front walk. She opened the door before we even knocked. This day was already amazing, and it had barely begun.

"Good morning!" Zoe shouted.

We laughed. "Good morning back," I said as she closed the door behind her.

"Don't you have to say bye to your mom and dad?" Bo asked.

Zoe tilted her head. "No, not really."

"Why?" he asked.

Her head stayed where it was. "I'm not sure."

"Why?" he asked again.

"I don't think I have them."

"Why?" yet again.

Tomorrow I was so asking Mom to take Bo to school.

"I live by myself," Zoe answered.

"Okay, enough about that," I said, trying to change the subject. "It's sunny outside. Who likes the sun? Yay, weather!"

Zoe and Bo laughed and started talking about how great spring was. I hung back and peered at

Zoe's little house over my shoulder. It looked so much like ours. Same brick exterior and bright red door. But instead of four people crammed inside of it, there was just her. I never really wrote about her family, or even mine all that much. So it made sense that she didn't have parents to live with. I never wrote them into life. She had no one telling her when to go to bed, what to eat, what chores to do. No one making her walk her annoying little brother to school. She could do anything she wanted, anytime.

I didn't want to admit that I'd been a little worried about having so much control over Zoe. But when she was home, the power was totally hers. I took a big breath, grinned, and hurried to catch up.

"Hey, can we talk?" A familiar voice stopped me by my locker.

"What's up?" I asked Clue.

"Well, I went to the pond last night and tried to get the magic to work for me, with my notebook, but it didn't happen. I think it might only work for one person at a time."

"Your notebook?" I'd seen him holding the same green one before, but I just figured it was for school stuff.

"Yeah." He held it up. "You're not the only one who writes, you know."

"What do you write about?"

I didn't know why I was curious. Could be a writer thing. Mrs. Yang says writing isn't just putting pen to paper: it's thinking, and planning, and talking about it with others too. Besides, he knew what I wrote about, so it was only fair that I got to know what he was writing about.

Clue looked at his shoes. "Oh . . . a person. Sort of like what you do. Anyway," he snapped back to attention, "it's okay that it didn't work yet, I guess. I should probably observe Zoe more and see how everything plays out before I try to bring my person into the world."

I raised my eyebrows at him. There were a lot of weird things about what he just said. *See how everything plays out?* Before he brings *his* person into the world? Did that mean he was going to swap Zoe out for somebody else? *What?*

I must have had a super stressed look on my face, because Clue shot me a reassuring smile.

"Look, I'm going to do my best to make this work out for both of us. I won't make Zoe disappear without talking to you first. Try to trust me, okay?"

Even with that smile, trusting him did not sound like the most possible thing in the world.

"Trust you? You stole my notebook!"

"But for a good reason! Besides, you didn't like me even before that," Clue said. "You're always glaring at me, even when I try to help you out. What did I ever do to you before now?" Clue looked seriously upset, and for a second I almost felt bad for him. But only for a second, and only the littlest bad feeling humanly possible.

"Yeah, you did something other than take my notebook," I told Clue. "Zoe is a better friend than you'll ever be, even if you do know all the answers to everything. And even if you somehow brought her to life." Then I slammed my locker shut and went to go find her. He obviously didn't remember that stealing my notebook wasn't the first bad thing he'd ever done.

At one of our first hospital visits, during the winter Dad started treatments, the nurse took all of us to this teeny chemo room with boring white walls and no windows. The staff had given Bo and me lollipops and told us how brave we were for going to chemo with Dad (which was pretty silly—we just had to sit there; he was the one who had to get poked and prodded and have all those tubey things stick-ing out of him).

"I don't want to be a bother," Mom had said to the nurse, "but last time we were here, we were in a room with a window. He likes looking out at the trees and the birds. It makes the time go a lot faster."

"Lila," Dad said softly, gently grabbing her wrist. "It's fine. Other people like the window seat too. It's not only us in here."

"I know." Mom said. "Every single person here deserves a freakin' window. When cancer is trying to get you, you should get a freakin' window."

She didn't exactly say *freakin'*, though.

I looked at the floor and pretended to be invisible. Bo clutched Giraffe and listened to Mom like she was telling the most suspenseful bedtime story of all time.

The vibe in that room got super weird then. The air seemed really heavy and it made my stomach feel so twisted and my brain so jumbly that I could hard-ly catch my breath. The walls hadn't seemed so bad to me at first, but suddenly it was like they were closing in and squishing me whole.

"I'm going to the bathroom," I croaked. I grabbed my notebook and rushed out of there as fast as I could.

That was when I saw him. Gresham Gorham, the kid at school with all the answers who'd been in Tiveda even longer than me. He was standing in front of a room on the other side of the hallway. A room that had a window.

And not just any window. A big one. With lots of birds and trees on the other side.

"Hi, Clue," I whispered.

"Hey," he said.

We stood there silently.

He pointed to my notebook. "Why are you always writing in that at school?" he asked.

I guess I was known for writing in my notebook like he was known for giving everyone clues in class.

The funny feeling in my stomach sped up to my throat. "My stories," I blurted out. "I write about a made-up girl named Zoe. We do a lot of fun stuff together. Like we sing and dance and hang out at the pond. We're sort of best friends."

My face turned red the second I said it. The fact that I didn't feel like myself, because of all the new Dad-having-cancer stuff didn't make it okay to just spill private information like that.

I tried to change the subject. "Are you here with your parents?"

"Yup," he said. His eyes stayed glued to my note-book. "My dad and my pops are around here some-where."

"Do they work here?"

"No . . . we're just . . . here," he said. For a guy so good at sharing hints, he sure wasn't giving anything away now.

I pointed behind him. "Are they somewhere in this giant room?"

He shook his head.

"So it's free?"

I let out a big breath as my whole body relaxed. How cool would it be if I could go back to Mom and Dad and Bo and tell them I got a room with a window?

But then Clue said, "No, it's not free."

"Oh."

And just like that, all of the seat-for-dad-by-the-window stuff went, well, right out the window.

I went back to our closet of a room and wrote stories while Bo and Giraffe drew pictures. Mom played classical music from her phone and stared at the walls, probably imagining how she'd like to open them up so Dad could see outside. Dad sat in the giant chair with all the tubey things and closed his eyes. He smiled, but he was sad. I could tell. I wasn't sure about what exactly. (The cancer? The walls? The picture Bo made of him defeating the bad guy where he kind of looked like a zebra?) Whatever it was, it made me sad too.

Eventually I had to go to the bathroom for real. It felt like hours since we'd gotten there. On my way I passed the room where I had seen Clue. Now the door was wide open, giving way to the emptiness inside. Clue stood in the doorway in the same firm position I'd seen him in before, like he was pretending he was a statue or a security guard or something.

"You said this room wasn't free." My voice came out crackly but sharp. He obviously just wanted to hang out in the best room while his parents were wherever they were. While my whole family was bored and miserable and squashed, he'd probably been watching TV, looking out the window, and having the time of his life.

"It wasn't free, and it still isn't."

I couldn't think of what to say back, so I didn't say anything at all. I just turned and walked away, with hot, uncomfortable anger thudding in my ears. We couldn't do much about Dad having cancer, but this room thing was a problem that had an easy solution. It was easy and it was there, and Clue, who said it was being used when it wasn't, had taken it away.

Back in the room Mom's face had lost the energy it had when we'd come in. She looked like she needed a nap, even though we'd been doing nothing all day. Dad's face had drooped too. And Bo's. We were one big sad family, and it was all Clue's fault.

For ages I'd been trying to push the memory out of my mind. But seeing Clue at school always reminded me why I would never be the president of his fan club, or even a member. Once again I tried to push the memory aside as I scanned the hall for Zoe. Clue brought her to life, and that was awesome. But that day at the cancer center might've been a little bit easier if we'd just had the better room.

14
Ready, Set, Shop

My heartbeat sped up with every step closer I got to her locker. I'd been with her on the walk to school, but it suddenly felt like hours had gone by, even days. I couldn't wait to see her, to talk to her, to laugh with her, all of it. I actually could not wait.

Only it looked like I would have to.

There was a giant crowd of people around Zoe at her locker. It seemed like almost every sixth grader was standing there—Sparkle Girls, non-sparkling girls, guys, everyone. Even teachers poked their heads out of their classrooms like they wanted to be part of whatever was going on. I stood at the edge of the crowd, trying to peek in to see what was going on. I finally gave up and pretended to tie my shoe, even though it was already in a super-solid double knot. Eventually everybody moved along, leaving Zoe all by herself.

"Jade!" She grinned at me and I forgot all about hospitals and rooms without windows.

"This school is the greatest," Zoe said. "Everybody's so nice. They were all worried about me after the liver incident yesterday. Even people who weren't in our class heard about it."

"That's so awesome," I said. "You're like, famous."

I watched as a few people walked by and gave Zoe high fives. I'd always imagined her as a popular person. It was pretty cool to see it happening.

Zoe closed her locker, and I linked my arm through hers. As we walked down the hall, heads turned and people stared, like we were actually walking down the red carpet on our way to the premier of our movie about being the Coolest Best Friends Ever in the history of best friends.

I, Jade Levy, not only had a real best friend. I had one everybody wanted. And she was all mine.

I lifted my head a little higher, and we kept on walking.

It got even better at lunchtime. I talked until my jaw got tired, laughed so hard I snorted, and apple juice came out of Zoe's nose. We almost forgot to eat.

Like yesterday, I couldn't believe it when it was time to go. It felt like we'd just sat down, like we'd blinked and now lunch was over.

It was the best feeling and the most disappointing one at the very same time.

"Word count?" Mrs. Yang asked as we walked by.

I shrugged and shot her a sheepish grin. *I tried, I swear,* I wanted to tell her. Even though that wasn't exactly the truth.

"What's she talking about?" Zoe asked.

"Oh, I used to write some of my stories about you at lunch," I said. "But hanging out with the real you is so much better."

"Hanging out with you is the best," she said. "You get me so well. But I guess that's because you invented me."

"Yeah," I agreed. I smiled to myself and tried to ignore the funny feeling in my stomach. It was pretty weird to hear her say that I'd *invented* her, like she was some kind of cool new app or game or something. But she was only saying the truth. I *had* invented her, and now I was helping her learn new things and have fun. And she was happy about it. We both were. But that didn't mean we had to talk about it all the time. As we walked into health, I made a mental note to write in my notebook that Zoe never mentions the whole being-invented thing again.

≈

"What are you doing after school?" I asked Zoe at the end of the day.

She gave me a funny look. Oh, right—she didn't know what she was doing after school. Because that, like everything else, was up to me.

"Hmm," I said. "We could hang out outside, but it's pretty windy today. Or we could go to the coffee shop, maybe."

I wasn't allowed to drink actual coffee, but everybody got those amazing blended drinks instead, with the whipped cream and the chocolate shavings on top, and there were really comfy chairs you could sit in while you drank them. It was a super-great place, even though it could only hold like five people at a time.

One of the Sparkle Girls, Afiya, whipped around in her seat. "Have you tried the new Mint Mocha Freeze?"

I folded my arms across my chest. Couldn't she see we were trying to talk, here? Privately?

"Sorry, I didn't mean to interrupt. I just love the coffee place so much. And those new mint mochas are my life. Zoe, you have to go there sometime. Do you like chocolate?"

"I . . . think so?" Zoe tilted her head and gave me a questioning look.

Afiya laughed before I could help Zoe out. We hadn't actually gotten to eat our chocolate-chip banana bread in that one story I'd written, but she totally would've liked it if she had the chance to take a bite.

"I know it's a complicated question," she continued. "Milk chocolate is my favorite, but dark chocolate is good too. And so is white chocolate, but it has to be the melt-in-your-mouth kind. It's best with lots of whipped cream."

Zoe made a face I didn't totally recognize.

"There are so many kinds of chocolate," she said. "I wonder which one I would like."

"Right? You'll have to eat little pieces of all of them sometime, one after the other. That's how I figured out my favorite." Afiya turned back around. Finally Zoe and I could get back to talking about our plans.

"We should go to the mall," I said as we packed up our stuff. I'd written this epic mall story a few months ago. Even though the mall was tiny, Zoe and I still had a ton of fun. If we went there today, our Best Mall Time Ever could happen for real—and this time, I could shop with actual money. Zoe and I could really buy things—special best-friend things—and take them home and keep them forever and ever.

"Yeah, let's go to the mall," Zoe agreed.

I smiled. "You're going to love it."

Zoe grinned. "I already do."

≈

After I called Mom from the office phone to make sure it was okay, Zoe and I made the short walk down the street until we were there. As much as I complained about Tiveda, it *was* nice how easy it was to get around. You could walk pretty much anywhere, and you didn't even need a parent to go with you most of the time. Which was especially good since I still didn't know how I was going to explain Zoe to Dad.

When we got to the mall, bright lights beat down on us like they were shining a giant spotlight over our heads. There were some other people around, but it felt like we were the only ones there. The mall was ours. It was ready. It was waiting. It was time.

Zoe grabbed my hand like she had in my story, and my skin tingled with excitement. It was like I was in the best dream ever, but it wasn't a dream at all. It was real life.

"Ready?" I asked.

"Set," she said.

"Shop," we yelled together.

We raced into the photo booth and took thousands of pictures making the funniest faces we could. We played on the mini indoor playground in the hallway between stores, even though it was technically for little kids. At Save-a-Lot, we bought a present for Bo and a new hat for Dad. We got gummy bears at the hardware store because they had really good candy. And then, finally, we went to Glimmer N' Gleam, because we were saving the best store for last.

We twirled around racks of clothes and jewelry and hair stuff and more. I always thought this mall was so dumb. But now, with Zoe, it was fun. Maybe places themselves weren't good or bad. Maybe it was the people you were with and the things you did that made places special.

"We should get matching bracelets," I told Zoe. I held up a couple beaded green ones. I had totally suggested this in my story, only now we could really get them. We could actually clasp them around each other's wrists and wear them everywhere for everyone to see. Whenever I felt sad or scared or any other feeling that was even the tiniest bit rotten, I could look at it and remember that I had a living, breathing best friend with the very same piece of jewelry around her arm.

I checked the price tag and thought about how much money I had left. I'd been saving up the money I made from watching Bo and helping out around the house forever, not for any real reason, just because there wasn't really anything I wanted to buy that bad until now, other than a blended drink from the coffee shop every now and then. After photos and the presents for Dad and Bo, I still had enough to get two bracelets and maybe even a couple little things from the clearance bin.

"Maybe we should get some hair stuff, too," I said. I grabbed a clip-on sparkly pink hair streak from the sale box. This wasn't part of my old story. In that story I never imagined that I'd have extra money. It was just one more way real life with Zoe was turning out to be even better than what I'd written.

I handed Zoe the hair clip, and she held it across her face like a mustache.

I giggled. She was so funny, even when she wasn't trying to be. "It goes up here," I said, and helped her attach it to the top of her head. Zoe spun around a few times and struck a funny pose.

We laughed as I stuck a few more clips to her head. I grabbed every different color and style I saw. It was hard to get them on there since she was spinning and dancing all goofy at the same time, but that's also what made it fun. I wrote about Zoe singing and dancing in most of my old stories, so it was no surprise that she was doing this now. Everyone else in the store was staring at us with huge smiles on their faces, like they had front-row seats to the greatest musical of all time.

I stood back as Zoe spun around faster and faster until she didn't even look like herself anymore—she just looked like this happy rainbow blur of joy and fun.

And that gave me an idea.

15

Mmmm, Carrots

"I'm home!"

Bo practically tackled me as soon as I opened the door.

"Jade! You didn't pick me up from school today," he said, as if I had no idea. "Mom picked me up in the truck, and Dad came too! And the truck defeated the bad guy. You should pick me up from school again soon. And then maybe one day *you* will be able to defeat the bad guy!"

I ruffled his hair. "I hope so. Hey, guess what? I brought you a present." I took out a brand-new set of crayons from my Save-a-Lot bag. There were only four in the box, but they were the fancy twisty kind where each crayon was actually two different colors. Bo's eyes practically popped out of his head.

"Do you like them?" I asked.

He grabbed them out of my hands and took off, so that seemed like a yes.

"Bo, *manners*," Mom called from the kitchen. He ran back and gave me a big hug.

"Thank you, Jade."

"Welcome," I said.

"Welcome," Zoe echoed.

We wandered into the living room. All of a sudden Mom appeared next to us. She was out of breath, like someone had chased her in here from the kitchen. Mom always seemed like someone was chasing her. She wiped some hair out of her face, set down the screwdriver in her hand, and shot Zoe a smile. "Who's this, Jadey?"

I twisted my hands together and rubbed them on my pants. Seriously, where did all this hand sweat come from whenever I was nervous? I could have totally normal hands—dry hands, even—and then, *bam*, they were the slimiest, slipperiest things ever.

I took a breath. It was now or never.

"This is my friend I went to the mall with," I

said. "Zoe. She's new at school. She actually lives right across the street."

Mom looked Zoe up and down, and I bit my tongue, hard. Once I had my idea at the mall, I'd used all my extra money to get as many cheap-o accessories as I could. Now Zoe was wearing a clip-on blue streak on one side of her head and a clip-on pink one on the other. She wore blue glasses that didn't really do anything for seeing but looked really cool, and a pair of very realistic-looking stick-on earrings above her real ones made it looked like her ears were double pierced. It was all kind of silly, but necessary too. Dad would never connect this Zoe to the one in my notebook.

"Nice to meet you, Zoe," Mom said. "I've been meaning to reach out to our new neighbors. Hope you and your family are enjoying it here so far."

"Zoe?" Dad said, shooting me a surprised look. "I didn't think that was a common name." Then he winked at me. *Whew.* Apparently Dad knew some sort of secret parent-kid code about *not* mentioning your daughter's imaginary best friend when her new real one with the same name shows up. Little did he know they were the *same* person.

I exhaled and let my tongue free.

"Check out what I got at the mall." I pulled it out of the bag and held it up. "Ta-da!"

The cap of the hat looked like half a basketball with a skinny black cylinder coming out of it. On top of that was a mini hoop. I went over to Dad's chair and handed it over, along with the teeny ball it came with.

"That," he said, "is amazing."

Mom laughed and started running in place. Then she swerved around an invisible member of the other team, dribbled an imaginary ball, and finally tossed a wiggly noodle through the hoop above Dad's head.

"Three pointer," she yelled, and pumped her fists in the air.

"Playing basketball together takes on a whole new meaning now," Dad said. He dropped the noodle into his mouth. "Thanks so much, Jade. Very thoughtful. This also makes eating extra convenient. Anyone want to throw a cookie in here?"

"Not before dinner." Mom wagged a joking finger at him. "Ten minutes till it's ready," she told us. She picked up the screwdriver she'd set down. "And, if we're lucky, we might have a fixed kitchen sink for dessert."

Bo giggled. "That's not a food." He turned to Zoe. "Want to help me make art?"

Zoe shot me a look, and I nodded. That weird pang from earlier slid back into my stomach. Was it weird that Zoe was looking to me to decide something like this? In some ways, shouldn't she just be her own person and make her own choices? I swallowed and tried to brush it off. It was fine. She was just trying to do the right thing, and I was trying to help.

"Totally," Zoe told Bo.

She flashed me a sideways smile and followed Bo to our room. I took a few more big breaths. The mall was so fun, and dinner would be too. But my heart was still beating too fast. What if Zoe's hair clips came out, or her fake glasses fell right off her face, or her sticky earrings unstuck? One little slip and Dad might realize that real Zoe and notebook Zoe were the same Zoe. And he'd freak out, and his cancer would probably come rushing back. Maybe I was being paranoid, but either way, I couldn't risk it.

So while Zoe did art projects with Bo, I took out my notebook and sparkly pencil, and I made sure Zoe wouldn't accidentally let her real identity slip.

≈

Zoe and Jade were having another super-fun day. School was great, the mall was amazing, and dinner would be pure awesomesauce. (Literally, because Mom was making pasta with her famous sauce.) Even though Zoe looked different now, her personality was the same. She was still friendly and outgoing, and Jade knew her family would love her.

At dinner, everybody had good, normal conversations. Zoe did the best job remembering that Jade's family—her dad especially—would be so confused and freaked out if they knew she was the Zoe from Jade's stories. She was totally up for helping to hide it however she could. So she made sure to keep her accessories in place.

It was the perfect end to another perfect day.

≈

I closed my notebook right as Mom was calling everybody to the table.

"Thank you for letting me stay," Zoe said once we were all seated. "This is so great. I'm so happy to be here."

Mom and Dad smiled at her and then at each other. A warm, fuzzy feeling overtook me. My parents were happy. Not worried. Not tired. Not stressed out. After all these zillions of years in Tiveda watching people come and go, their daughter finally had a real best friend in the world and she was at the table. Now everybody could relax. Maybe even me.

"I can eat spaghetti with my ears," Bo told Zoe. "Watch."

"Bo." Mom made a face, and he put the noodle down.

"Fine," he said. "But I really can."

"I believe you," Zoe said. She munched on some roasted carrots and got this look on her face like she was in food heaven. "These are amazing! Wow. Wow. Wow. These are the most delicious orange sticks I have ever had in my entire life."

I coughed. *Orange sticks?* Pretty sure they were the only orange sticks (aka carrots) she'd ever had in her entire life, but Mom and Dad probably didn't need to know that.

I snuck a peek at my parents. They looked more entertained than anything else, but we were one second away from who-is-this-girl-and-why-does-she-not-seem-to-know-what-carrots-are questions.

So I did the only thing I could do—I lifted some carrots to my mouth in a super-excited, I-could-total-ly-be-in-a-commercial-for-carrots-in-fact-Zoe-and-I-are-actually-performing-one-right-now kind of way.

"Mmmm, carrots," I said.

Zoe's eyes lit up. "Carrots!" she repeated. "What a word! What a food!"

"They're the carrot-y-iest carrots in the world," I added.

Everybody erupted into laughs. I leaned back in my seat and took a breath. Okay. Our secret was safe for now.

"How was kindergarten today, Bo?" Zoe asked once everyone calmed down.

"So fun!" He threw a handful of spaghetti noodles in the air, and Mom gave him another look. It was one thing to throw a noodle at Dad's hat or to threaten to eat it with your ears. It was a little different to basically dump a handful on the floor. "It's confetti," he explained. "For celebration of fun kindergarten."

I looked at Zoe, and she looked at me, her eyes gleaming. Without saying a word, we both burst into laughter.

OPPSERVATION: Sometimes perfect nights don't look perfect. Your best friend wears a goofy disguise and goes bonkers for carrots. Food ends up all over the floor, and you have to help clean *it up even though you weren't the one who made the mess.*

Questions for further research: Why can't every night be this unexpectedly good?

But of course it couldn't just stay that way.

"Hey, Jade," Dad called to me before bed. "What are the chances, after all this time, that you'd actually make a friend named Zoe? Pretty funny, right?"

It felt wrong to try to lie or agree that it was so super funny. So instead of saying anything, I bent down and hugged him again.

"Night, Dad."

He squeezed me as tight as he could, which wasn't very tight at all.

"Night, Jade."

16
School Supplies and Other Major Dangers

I woke up the next day with a big smile on my face. Our night was so fun. Talking about carrots, playing board games after dinner . . . even helping Bo clean up noodles was fun. My smile stayed on at school too. Nothing could bug me today. Not Clue, not Sparkle Girls, not health class or any class. I could walk into a field of sharks and vampires and they might as well all be covered in rainbows and butterflies and spaghetti confetti. I had no doubt that today would be as amazing as yesterday. Maybe even more.

And it was—until I got to English and Mrs. Yang called me up to her desk.

"Hey, Jade. I wanted to see how the writing's going this week."

Oh, hello, sweaty hands and desert-dry mouth. I was so getting busted for my zero-word days. But actually, maybe that wasn't entirely true. Just because I hadn't written at lunch lately didn't mean I hadn't written at all.

"Pretty good," I said. "I've been writing a lot at home. Like, *a lot* a lot." I peeked over my shoulder to check on Zoe. I was a tiny bit worried she might get confused by erasers or rulers or highlighters or something. Last night after she went home, I'd gone through my old stories and made a list of things she knew about, and those were *not* on the list, just like carrots. What if she tried to sharpen her pencil and accidentally sharpened a finger instead?

"Oh, yeah? I'm glad to hear it," Mrs. Yang said. I forced myself to look back at her, but it felt like there was some kind of magnetic force that wanted me to watch Zoe instead. "You're a real writer, you know," Mrs. Yang added. "Writers have to write no matter what else is going on in their lives. They always make the time."

"Sorry, what?" Taking a super-short peek behind me revealed that Zoe and Afiya were talking. Not that that was a problem. But I probably needed to get over there soon.

"I mainly wanted to see if you're all right," she continued. "You've seemed a little distracted this week."

I made myself look her in the eye. Today her typical warm smile felt more annoying than comforting. "I'm good," I said quickly. "Really. Just busy. I feel like my main character is depending on me, you know?"

Mrs. Yang nodded. "It's good to write characters who feel real," she said. "They do depend on you, in a way. But sometimes it's the other way around, and writers depend on their characters. They get so caught up in their work that they can't tell where their stories end and real life begins." She tapped her nails against her desk. "Believe it or not, it's actually good for writers to take a break every now and then. Writers have to write, of course, but they should also spend time being present in their lives."

"*Mmhmm.* Totally." Usually I was super into whatever writing advice Mrs. Yang wanted to share, but this little tidbit seemed pretty obvious. Like, yeah, writers get really into their stories. Duh. They should. And of course they should do stuff in real life too. That's exactly what I was doing: writing Zoe and then hanging out with Zoe. So it was like, *Thanks, Mrs. Yang, but also please stop talking so I can go write more and make sure my not-so-fictional character does what she needs to do.*

Finally, after what felt like the longest conversation ever, Mrs. Yang waved her hand like, *Okay, whatever, moving on,* and told me I could be seated. I raced over to Zoe instead.

"Hi," she said. I took a long breath. She hadn't chopped off any fingers or anything while I was gone, it looked like, so that was a relief.

"Hey." I twirled a piece of hair around my finger. "Sorry I got called away to talk to the teacher."

"Oh, no problem. Gave me a chance to hang out with Afiya a little."

My throat tightened. "Cool. What were you talking about?"

Zoe shrugged. "I don't know. Food, mostly. Afiya says there are a lot of things I need to try."

I tried to smile, but my mouth wouldn't do it. What was my deal? It was good Zoe wanted to try what Afiya recommended. If that led to her wanting to try other new things, that'd be good too. It would only be a problem if it led to her wanting to try other best friends.

As Mrs. Yang started class, I grabbed my pencil and notebook.

School could be kind of a danger zone, sometimes. There were things that could hurt you. A lot of them were school supplies. (Seriously, who decided staplers were a good idea? There had to be a better way to hold a bunch of papers together.) But all kinds of things could hurt. People could hurt you too. Words could. And at school, people, words, and school supplies were everywhere.

Luckily Zoe was smart and careful. She liked learning new things and meeting new people, but she checked with Jade before she did anything. That way, she could make sure that she went home happy each day, with all her fingers and nothing stapled together that shouldn't be. She really appreciated how Jade always looked out for her. Even though there were a bunch of other people around who could sometimes be sort of interesting, she knew Jade was the only best friend she needed.

Mrs. Yang announced that we were going to have free-writing time, so I kept going.

Zoe started going over to Jade's house for dinner every night. It seemed like everybody was happier when she was around. Jade's mom was happy that she had someone new to test recipes on, Jade's dad was happy that he could finally wear hats more than once because they'd be new to Zoe, Bo was happy that he had someone new to draw pictures of defeating the bad guy, and Jade was happy that everyone else was happy. Plus, she was regular happy too.

Even after hanging out for hours night after night, Zoe and Jade never got sick of each other, they never got bored, and they never thought about what it would be like to hang out with anybody else. When they were together, they forgot about everything else going on in the world—things like Jade's dad's cancer and the fact that they lived in a town full of dead flowers and weird, magical water—and concentrated only on fun. After Zoe went home and Jade climbed into bed, totally wiped out, they'd miss each other, even though they knew they'd see the other again the next morning.

OPPSERVATION: It was hard to miss someone you got to see so much.

Questions for further research: Why did I even think about missing Zoe at the same time that we were having the most fun we'd ever had?

I looked at what I'd written. They were just messy words scribbled on a page, just hopes and dreams and ideas, but they would become reality soon enough. Zoe had told me to be specific, after all, and I had delivered. I turned around to look at her. Without really knowing what I was thinking about, she grinned at me. Then she put down the scissors she was playing with. *Whew.* (Where did she even get scissors? It was seriously a good thing I was around.)

At the end of class Mrs. Yang announced that she'd like everyone to pass in their free-write, so she could take a peek at what we'd been working on.

My heart raced. Pass it in? I'd written in my notebook, and there was no way I was letting that out of my sight again.

I trailed behind everyone on the way out. Some kids handed over loose papers, while others set their notebooks on Mrs. Yang's desk.

"Um, would it be okay if I didn't share this time around?" I asked Mrs. Yang.

"Well, I noticed you writing quite a bit today," she said. "I'd love to see what you're working on so intently."

I bit my lip. This smelled fishy. Was this her

sneaky teacher way of trying to get me to do what she said and take a break and focus on my actual life? She didn't understand that this notebook, these words, they *were* my life. They were Zoe's life too.

"You can just rip out some pages if you don't want to give me your whole enormous notebook," she offered.

I tilted my head to the side. That was better, but it wasn't going to work either. It sounded too risky. The pages probably needed to stay in my notebook in order to work in real life.

"Can you make a copy?" I asked. Teachers were always talking about making copies. It seemed like something they really enjoyed.

Mrs. Yang raised an eyebrow. "I guess so," she said.

"Awesome! I'll wait here," I told her.

She gave me a funny look, but she left the room with my notebook. When she came back a couple minutes later, she had a copy of today's work for her and a fully intact yellow notebook for me.

I breathed out and hugged it tight. Even though her advice this morning was way off, I still wanted to be an author someday. It would probably be smart to hear what she thought of my writing.

"Thanks for sharing this with me," she said. "I can't wait to see what you've been working on."

"Just so you know," I warned her, "the story is sort of . . . real . . . and magical. Like, things happen that wouldn't normally happen in our world. So if you notice anything about, I don't know, magical water or something, just go with it, okay? Also, it's based on people I know."

Mrs. Yang nodded. "Noted," she said. "I'm looking forward to it."

I smiled to myself, thinking of the story coming true.

"Me too," I said.

17
Tater Tots With A Side of Sparkles

At lunch Zoe and I took our usual spots across from each other at our regular table, and she inspected everything on her tray.

"Are these Tater Tots?" she asked, in the same kind of voice you might use to ask, *Is that million dollars for me?*

"They sure are," I said. We'd had them together in a story before, so unlike carrots, she basically knew what they were.

"Tater Tots!" she repeated.

"Tater Tots!" I tried to match the level of excitement in her voice.

"Tater Tots!" she said again.

"Tater Tots Tater Tots Tater Tots," I answered.

It wasn't one of the most interesting conversations we'd ever had, but it was definitely one of the goofiest, and that was just as good.

"Tater Tots Tater Tots," she told me.

"Tater—"

"Um, hi?"

I looked up. Who would dare interrupt this obviously super-important conversation?

Afiya smiled. The rest of the Sparkles stood behind her with their trays. They all had something sparkly on—a headband, a necklace, a belt, you name it. Even Afiya's hijab was made out of a shimmery green fabric.

The Sparkle Girls were always coming and going, like everyone else in this town. Somehow there were always more members to keep the group going. And no matter who was in the group, they never seemed to want to include me in it.

I tried to smile back at Afiya, but I was really confused at why they were standing there.

"Can we sit with you, Zoe?" Scarlett asked.

Oh.

"And with you, Jade?" Afiya added.

Gee, thanks.

Zoe grinned. "Hi! That would be—" she glanced my way, and before I even realized what I was doing, I shook my head the teeniest bit. A tiny part of me may have wanted to sit with them before, but not now that I had Zoe. It was obvious that they only wanted to hang out with her, not me. Still, telling them they couldn't sit with us was kind of mean. Shaking my head a tiny bit was still shaking my head. I opened my mouth to change my mind, but Zoe spoke up first. "That would be not the best thing right now, I guess," she said. "I'm sorry. But I hope you have an amazing lunch. Have you seen these Tater Tots? They're the greatest, right? Almost better than orange—I mean, carrots!"

Afiya laughed. "You're the funniest, Zoe. Maybe we can eat together tomorrow. We need to figure out what kind of chocolate you like!"

Then the Sparkles turned and walked away.

A bad feeling bubbled up in my throat. Why'd I have to shake my head like that? I wouldn't like it if people shook their heads about me. But at the same time, when the Sparkles left, I couldn't help feeling something like . . . relief.

"So, as we were saying." I smiled. "Tater Tot Tater Tot Ta—"

"Why did you shake your head like that?" Zoe interrupted. "I . . . they seem cool, I think, right? I like people. And there are open seats by us."

The inside of my mouth went desert-dry. I knew she was right. But it wasn't like they had to go sit on the floor now or something like that. There were open seats all over the place. There were open seats at the tables by the garbage cans and by the milk line and a few at the table where Clue sat with a few girls from science . . . there were even some close to the door, which is the best place to be because then you get to leave first and beat all the walking traffic. Seats were everywhere. So couldn't they go sparkle over in one of those places instead?

"I don't know," I answered honestly. I twirled some hair around a sweaty finger. "But there are lots of places they can sit. So everything's okay. Right?"

"I know," said Zoe, "but I think they wanted to sit with us. And talk to us. And be friends and stuff. Like we are."

"Yeah, but . . ." I looked around and tried to think of something to say, but my mind was a total blank. Spotting Clue eyeballing us didn't help my brain work better, either. He usually sat in different places, but no matter where he sat lately, he always seemed to be watching Zoe and me like a mad scientist back at the pond. It was awesome having her here, of course, but he had no idea just how tricky it was turning out to be.

Everything had been going so great—and still was, really—so why did I feel like somebody had dropped a bucket of old, soggy Tater Tots on my head?

"We don't need them," I said after a too-long silence. "It's better when it's just the two of us."

Zoe sipped her chocolate milk and looked like she was thinking about it.

"Yeah, I guess you're right. We don't need more friends."

I sat up a little straighter and drank my milk too. It tasted extra chocolatey and delicious, and for a second I didn't have that Tater-Tots-on-my-head-messy-greasy-icky feeling. Until I looked over at Zoe and saw that she was staring at the Sparkles, and the bad feeling came rushing back.

18
The Stuff That Matters

After school we picked up Bo and walked home the same way we had a couple days before, with the swinging and the shouting and the laughing. After the way Zoe had looked at the Sparkles earlier, it was extra important that this afternoon was the most fun one yet.

We were almost home when Zoe said, "You can come to my house today, if you think that's a good idea. It could be fun, maybe. Right?"

I bit the inside of my lip. Yeah. It probably would be fun. After all, Zoe didn't have any parents around to tell her what to do or not to do or to make her feel sad. (Not that Dad did that to me on purpose, but still.) I straightened my shoulders. Yeah, why didn't we go to her house? Just because we'd never been there in my stories didn't mean it was impossible. It just hadn't happened yet.

"Let's do it," I said.

"Let's do it!" Bo agreed.

I shot Zoe an *uh-oh* kind of look, and she made one back.

"I think this is going to be, um, big-kid time," I said. By the look on Bo's face, I knew I'd said the wrong thing.

"I *am* a big kid," he insisted.

"I know," I said. "Sorry. I mean . . . bigger kids."

"Oh." He nodded slowly. "Okay. But if the bad guy comes . . ."

"We'll call you," I promised.

He smiled as we crossed the street to our house. I opened the door, let him in, and called for Mom.

"We're going to hang out at Zoe's today, if that's okay," I told her.

She smiled. "Sure. Actually I've been meaning to go over and introduce myself to her parents. Maybe I'll come with you for a second."

"NO!" I yelled. "I mean, no thanks," I said in a calmer voice, even though I was sweating out of pretty much every single body part. "It's not a good time right now. Her dad's at work, and her mom . . . her mom lost her voice."

"Yeah," Zoe said. "My mom can't find her voice. It could be anywhere."

"Too much singing," I added.

It felt bad to lie, but we had to do it.

Mom gave us a funny look. "Okay," she said slowly, "I'll try to catch them another time. Be home in time for dinner."

"We will be!" Zoe answered.

I put one hand on the door and the other on Zoe's backpack. "Okay," I said. And with a light, friendly, *please-hurry-up* tug, we were out of there.

We giggled the whole way across the street.

"And then you were like, *She lost her voice!*" she said, and we cracked up all over again. It wasn't like I was proud of lying to Mom, but it was nice having another thing only my best friend and I knew.

Zoe opened the door and tossed her backpack on the ground. At my house, I usually tossed my backpack on the couch. But as I looked around, I realized . . . there was no couch.

There was also no table. No chairs. No lamps or plants or rugs. There were no typical living room things whatsoever.

The room wasn't empty, though. Far from it. There was a giant stuffed unicorn in the corner, next to a bunch of empty pizza boxes. In my stories, Zoe liked eating homemade meals at my house, because she mostly ordered pizza at hers. There was a bike, a box of sparkly pencils, a couple pairs of shoes, a huge umbrella, and a giant sled.

All of the objects looked so familiar.

"So, what do you want to do?" Zoe asked. She plopped onto a weirdly-shaped blanket. It was like whoever made it was trying to make a rectangle but made a much different shape instead. There were places where it was uneven, and other spots where bunches of stuffing were spilling out. It looked like something a little kid had made.

Wait a second. I looked closer. A little kid *had* made it—me!

I remembered now. It was the summer after fourth grade. Dad called it my Sewing Phase, which I thought was not very nice because I was going to sew forever. I hadn't really sewn since, but that was beside the point. In real life I made presents for everybody—mostly tiny, weird-shaped blankets, because that was all I knew how to make. One for Mom, one for Dad, one for Bo, one for Bo's stuffed giraffe. And then, in a story, I wrote about making one for Zoe.

"Whoa," I said out loud. I pulled my glasses down and looked out over the rims. These weren't random objects in Zoe's house. These were things from my stories. Things I'd written about Zoe and I buying together or making together or things I'd given her to take home. They were on my "Things Zoe Knows" list. And now here they were, all spread out like they were in a museum. The things she knew. The things she owned. The life I'd made her.

"Whoa," she repeated. I blinked and tried to smile, even though seeing all this stuff was super weird. I wondered—if I wrote a new story where Zoe suddenly got a bunch of new things, would that stuff actually show up here?

I shook my head and let the thought fall out. No. My friendship with Zoe wasn't about stuff. I didn't care what she had, and she didn't care what I had. We had each other. If there was something she really wanted, I could see if I could get it. But otherwise, everything we needed was right here.

"So what do you want to do?" she asked again.

I looked around at all the random things. They were all part of our story. Instead of making new stories right now, I just wanted to be with the fun, familiar past. "Let's take a walk down memory lane," I said.

Zoe stood up. "Okay. Let me get my shoes. Is Memory Lane by the mall?"

I laughed. "Not quite." I linked my arm through hers. "Come on. Let's look through all your stuff."

≈

"Where's Dad?" I asked as we all sat down to eat. Zoe and I had come back to my house in time for dinner, just like we promised Mom we would.

Mom set two big dishes on the table and hurried to pull something else out of the oven. "Oh. Dad's, um, having dinner in bed tonight."

"Why?" Bo asked.

"Because it's fun."

"Why?" he asked again.

"Because," Mom said, "it's like breakfast in bed, but at dinnertime. Everybody should get a meal in bed every once in a while."

I waited for Bo to ask why again, but he seemed cool with that answer.

"Can tomorrow be my turn?" he asked.

Mom smiled. A relieved look flashed onto her face but quickly disappeared. "Maybe," she said.

I stared at the yummy lasagna and garlic bread on the table. I'd been hungry, but now, not so much. Dad had dinner in bed a few times before, but it wasn't just for fun, it was because he was so tired that he couldn't even sit at the table for the time it took to eat. Even though the cancer was supposed to be gone, actually feeling better could take forever.

"Hey." Zoe nudged me with her elbow, and I looked up. Her green eyes watched me like they were trying to tell me something. She smiled gently and poked my arm a few times, and I knew exactly what she was saying. *I get it. It's scary. We don't have to talk about it if you don't want to. And I'm here no matter what.*

The temperature in the room hadn't changed, but goosebumps prickled up all over my skin. Zoe was saying the same thing she'd said to me that one summer day when Mom told me not to worry them with anything. Only now she wasn't saying it from the pages of a notebook—she was saying it for real, with real eyes and a real smile.

I closed my eyes and dropped my head onto her

shoulder. I thought about the weirdness during lunch earlier today. Maybe the Sparkles got Zoe to notice them then, but for the stuff that really mattered—stuff like after-school fun and our family dinners—she was still mine.

19
The Right Words

The next day at lunch, Afiya and the Sparkles appeared in front of our table, just like I secretly hoped they wouldn't. They smiled at Zoe and I fidgeted in my seat. Yeah, she was funny and fun and nice and popular and smart, but come on, so were other people!

Okay, if I were them, maybe I'd try to sit with her too.

But still.

"So, I brought every kind of chocolate from home," Afiya told us. "Taste-test time?"

Zoe fiddled with her fingers. She stared at her hands. She looked at me, and when I didn't say or do anything, she mumbled, "Sure."

I bit my lip as Afiya sat down on my right. Scarlett took the spot to my left, and Janelle and Camila sat on the other side. The table became so loud so fast that I could barely hear Zoe—or the thoughts zooming through my own head.

This was fine. This was totally fine. They could sit here. Zoe and I were still best friends, and we'd get time alone together later. Plus, I still felt bad for shaking my head yesterday. Anyway, I'd written that she was popular, so what did I expect?

Then again, I'd also written that despite her popularity, she only wanted to hang out with me.

As the conversation continued around me, I mindlessly combed through the food on my tray with my spork. What if Zoe somehow forgot that I was the only friend she needed? I was the only one who really knew her, the only one who'd been there for her even before she turned real.

I thought of the notebook sitting in my bag all lonely. And I realized: there was a way to make sure she remembered.

"I'll be right back," I said, not that anyone was listening.

I grabbed a spot at a mostly-open table and flipped to a new page, but before I could bring my pencil to the paper, Clue plopped down beside me.

"Um, hi?"

"Hey," he said. "What's up? Seems like things are going pretty well with your surprise."

"Yeah," I said. Part of me considered sharing how certain things could go better, but that sounded like the kind of thing you talk about with a friend. Which Clue wasn't. I was pretty sure that giving somebody something—even if it was the best surprise ever—didn't mean they automatically had to be your friend.

"Good," he said. "That notebook really took to the water," he added, tapping the blank page staring up at us. "I just can't believe she was right about the pond being magical. I always hoped it was true, especially lately, but it seemed like something we just imagined and daydreamed about, you know?"

I didn't answer.

We sat silently for a few seconds. I didn't have the energy to ask Clue what in the heck he was rambling about again. Clue opened his mouth every now and then like he wanted to say something, but then he changed his mind. I tapped on my notebook with my pencil. I really needed to write, but no way was I going to do it with him sitting right here watching.

For someone so good at giving hints, he wasn't the best at taking them.

"Clue, thanks for checking in," I finally said, "but I really need to get back to writing."

"Oh," he said. "Yeah, sure."

He got up and blinked a bunch, almost like he was in some kind of daze. He scanned the cafeteria like he wasn't totally sure what or who he was looking for. But eventually he wandered over to a table of people from our math class and took a seat, and I started to write.

Zoe was just being polite to the Sparkle Girls. Her manners were great. In fact, that was one of the trillions of reasons she liked hanging out at Jade's: so she could share her great manners with Bo, who still had a lot of them left to learn.

Someone made a throat-clearing sound, and I looked up.

Zoe stared back at me. Her arms swung by her sides and a frown seemed frozen to her face. I didn't think I'd ever seen Zoe frown before. It made my stomach flip over and fall back down with a big, messy *splat*.

"Are you mad at me?" she asked. "I'm sorry I said they could sit with us. It's just that you didn't tell me what to do, and I didn't think saying no made any sense. I wanted . . ." she paused, and a small smile crossed her face for a second. "I wanted to say yes. But did you want me to say no? Can you explain, like, why we should say no? I want to understand."

I lowered my gaze and tried to ignore the tightness in my chest.

The thing was . . . yeah, I wanted her to say no, but that was mean. I didn't want to admit feeling that way. I didn't want to feel that way, period. I couldn't explain why. There was no real reason to say no. It was mostly a feeling that had made me shake my head yesterday, and feelings were hard to talk about, sometimes, especially ones that didn't make you feel very proud of yourself. Zoe was supposed to understand this like she always had. Unlike Nessa or any of my other former best friends, Zoe was supposed to just *get it,* no matter what it was. She was supposed to be my friend no matter what, even if I said or did the wrong thing, like left her birthday party early or stumbled when I tried to explain the reason.

It seemed like a million years passed as Zoe stood there watching me and I sat there trying to figure out what to say. But I couldn't think of a good way to answer, so I finally told her, "I'm not mad at you," and went back to looking at my notebook.

"Well . . . I might go back over there, then, if that's okay."

I nodded, even though I practically had to grab my neck to get it to cooperate.

"Cool. I'll see you in health, then."

Zoe backed away slowly, like she was waiting to see if I would say something more. But I still couldn't think of the right words to say—or to write—so I slumped down, dropped my pencil, and tried not to watch her go. My story said she was just being polite to them, but it felt like she really, truly liked Afiya and the Sparkles.

I stared at my feet and tried not to let myself wonder if she could ever end up liking them more than me.

≈

"Word count?"

I shrugged at Mrs. Yang.

"I wrote, but it's not very good."

"What do you mean?"

"I don't know. It's hard to write the right thing all the time."

Mrs. Yang smiled, but there was nothing happy about my writing—and life—problems.

"I know how that goes," she said. "Remember, there's no need to stress too much about first drafts," she added. "They don't need to be amazing. They just need to exist."

I frowned. Mrs. Yang's advice was getting more frustrating by the day.

"I know," I said again. "But I just really need some first drafts to be perfect."

"I understand that it feels that way," Mrs. Yang said, "but do great piano players or athletes or surgeons just wake up that way? No, it takes practice. And with writing, practice is more than writing first drafts. It's taking what you have and making it better, just like basketball players adjust different things about their free throws and their shots improve. Believe me—no one ever gets everything exactly the way they want it in a first draft. Not even professional authors. That's what revision is for."

I bit my lip. An author told us that in a video chat once. And so maybe that was true in general, but these circumstances were a little unusual.

"And hey, Jade, it's okay to not write the perfect story even after you revise. Like the story you gave me yesterday—I had a chance to look at it, and it has a lot of potential. I was mainly looking to see that everyone is writing, but if you're open to feedback, I definitely have some ideas for ways you can revise. And then there may be some things you decide on your own that you want to change. It can be an ongoing process. What matters most is that you've done the best work you possibly can and you're proud of what you've created."

I tucked some hair behind my ears and leaned against the wall. "But what if I still explain something wrong, or my characters say the wrong thing, or I don't give enough details?"

I thought about lunch. I should've written that Zoe talked to me for longer until she got me to say something smart and clever that captured my confused feelings. I should've written something more than what I did.

"Then that's okay," Mrs. Yang said, jerking me out of my thoughts. "Jade, listen to me. If you provided every single little piece of information about your characters in your stories, there'd be nothing left for your readers to imagine. And you'd end up writing an encyclopedia instead of a book. I like books that ask me to fill in the blanks and come up with my own answers to some of the questions that arise. I think that's a lot more fun than being bogged down by a bunch of specifics." She paused. "You know, writing is choosing which words to use. But it's also choosing which words to leave out."

A sudden lightness draped over me like a cozy sweater on a chilly day. "So writing can be . . . not writing?" I asked.

Mrs. Yang laughed. "I think it's mostly about trusting your readers. They'll figure out the things you don't tell them. And maybe they will imagine things about your characters and plot that are more amazing than anything you would have imagined yourself."

I smiled and repeated her words in my head. *Trust your readers.*

Maybe Mrs. Yang's advice wasn't perfect lately, but this thought was pretty good.

Zoe wasn't reading my stories exactly, but somehow, her brain was. So maybe I had to trust her to come up with some of her own answers and storylines. If I tried to write every little thing, I'd drive myself bonkers . . . kind of like I was doing now.

It sounded impossible. But maybe sometimes every author had to let go of getting it totally right.

Even me.

20
Partner Projects

r. Kremen smiled at us as soon as the bell rang for fifth period to start.

"So back to our friend the liver," he said, and everybody groaned, except for Zoe, who laughed.

"I'm not eating that stuff again," she called out, and everyone else laughed too.

"No one expects you to," he said. "No more liver here. We're almost done with the whole digestive system, as a matter of fact. To finish it up, we're going to do a final project in pairs. You can choose any aspect of the digestive system you'd like, any part or process, and demonstrate what you've learned about it in a creative way. This will be due next Friday."

Ugh. That sounded about as fun as lunch had been. But at least the project was with partners, so that was good. Maybe I'd get to work with Zoe, and we'd have to work on it at lunch! Then the Sparkles really couldn't sit with us. It was the perfect excuse.

But before I could think any more about how great it was that we had partners for this, Mr. Kremen started assigning them.

"Thea and Evelyn, Logan and Levi, Jordan and Remy, Jonah and Mikah . . ." I crossed my fingers and my toes and tried to cross my eyes, too, only that never really worked. It usually just made my head hurt. I kept trying anyway. "Zoe and Afiya, Jade and Gresham, Maggie and Keyaris, Alexa and Ariella, Ethan and Jackson . . ."

As Mr. Kremen continued with the list, my heart felt like it had fallen to my feet and rolled right out the door. A funny noise came out of my throat as Zoe and Afiya grinned at each other from across the room. Trust her, I told myself in a very firm silent voice. *Trust her!*

That was going to be easier said than done.

Mr. Kremen gave us a few minutes to meet with our partners, so I peeled my eyes away from Zoe and Afiya and made my way over to Clue.

"Did you do something?" I blurted out.

"I've done a lot of things," he said. "Today alone, I ate breakfast and lunch, went to class and the library . . ."

I glared at him. "Clue."

He smirked. "Oh, was that not what you meant?"

"It's Zoe," I whispered. "Things are just being weird today."

My face burned as I caught his eye. I didn't know why I kept blurting things out to Clue, but there it was.

"Forget it," I said.

Clue's face was serious now. "No, tell me," he said. "What's going on?"

I sighed. I really didn't want to talk to Clue about this, but I couldn't talk to Zoe about it. Or Mom or Dad, obviously. He was sort of my only option.

A big gulp traveled down my throat. "So, I'm sure you already know that the things I write about Zoe . . . happen," I said. "But lately she's not following all of my, um, storylines. At first it seemed like she said or did almost everything I wrote. And she still is, but she's doing a lot of other things, too, and making more friends, and saying things I didn't write. I know I need to trust her, and I want to, but it's . . . hard."

He tapped a pencil to his chin. "I figured as much about the writing. Nobody just sings 'Twinkle, Twinkle' like that. Anyway, that's probably how it's going to be. She's going to do things you don't write, unless you narrate every single moment of her life."

Hmm. That wasn't a terrible idea. Except that it would probably be a ton of work. There were zillions of things that happened each day, and even though a lot of them weren't that important or interesting, I'd have to keep track of every single one. I'd have to start first thing in the morning and stay up all night. And I'd have to do it, like, every night, since each day was a teeny bit different than the last. I had to do what Mrs. Yang said, at least when it came to that. I didn't have to provide every single detail. I had to trust that my readers—that Zoe—would fill in the blanks.

But what if, for some reason, I couldn't trust her? What if her filling in the blanks was exactly what I was afraid of?

"What's so bad about her deciding what she wants to say and do anyway?" Clue asked. "Real people do that. And you like that she's a real person now, don't you? When it's my turn to use the magic, and my secret comes to life, I'll stay out of it and let my person be herself, do what she wants."

My mouth turned to sandpaper as I remembered how the magic could only work for one person at a time. "Please don't switch," I whispered.

"I won't . . . yet." He raised an eyebrow, and I looked away. "We can talk more about that later," he added. "We only have a few minutes, and we should discuss our project. I think we should study the liver."

I frowned. *Of course* he wanted to study the liver. There were a ton of digestive parts to choose from, but that was the one he wanted for our project?

"I'd rather not," I said.

"I don't know about you, but I like to learn more about the things I don't understand," he said, "and the things that scare me."

I understood the stupid liver fine. And I so wasn't scared of it. Who would be scared of a big squishy blob?

And even if I was scared of it (not that I was), how would he know that, and why would he care?

"Just think about it," he said. He turned to the green notebook on his desk. "Think about everything."

"Fine," I said. But I didn't mean it one bit.

21
Perfect Moments

After school I tried not to think about how Afiya had decided that she and Zoe had to work on their project. They were going to the school library while I went to get Bo. When they were done, Zoe would come to my house for dinner. It was a good enough plan, but any plan that involved Zoe hanging out with Afiya—or anyone who wasn't me—was not a plan I was super excited about.

I knew I couldn't tell Zoe what to do and say every single second. Mrs. Yang's advice about that was right, and so was Clue's, even though I didn't want to admit it. The fact was it'd be too much like writing a long list of all the boring, everyday things. My hands would get crampy and tired, even if I typed every word. Maybe I had to be better at noticing our perfect best-friend moments, the simple ones that made me happy. Maybe I'd keep a better eye out for them.

And maybe I'd write a few, just in case, but with things Zoe could fill in.

≈

It was a normal night at Jade's house. Her dad was wearing a camo hat—"Camo—not to be confused with chemo!" he'd announced earlier. Her mom was cleaning and organizing and fixing things and painting and cooking all at the same time. Bo was sprawled out on his stomach, holding Giraffe with one hand and drawing what looked like an octopus defeating the bad guy with the other. Zoe was next to him, helping, and Jade was on the couch. In a few minutes, Jade decided, they were going to play cards—the game where you slap your hand on the pile when there's a match—and they were both going to slap at the same time. They were going to start giggling, and they were going to keep moving their hands so they were stacking them on top of each other's over and over and over again, faster and faster and faster. They'd giggle harder and harder, and finally they'd get tired and stop. Then, without any words, they'd look at each other and start messing up all the cards, the ones in the pile and the ones in their hands. And Zoe would lean back and say something about how great this was. Jade would nod, and they'd smile at each other using only their eyes, because eyes could smile as much as actual smiles could. It would be exactly what they needed.

Mom rushed by with a spatula in her hand. "Ten minutes till dinner," she said. By now Mom pretty much expected that Zoe would eat with us. Zoe could actually look like herself too. No nightly disguise needed! I wasn't so worried about Dad making the connection now that I wasn't really sharing my stories.

"Want to play cards?" I asked in a way-too-excited kind of voice.

Zoe gave me a funny look. "Sure."

We lay across from each other on the floor and I did my best to play it cool. There wasn't anything to be nervous about, so why were my hands doing their annoying sweaty thing?

"Afiya told me that famous musicians used to

play in Tiveda, back in the olden days," Zoe said as she dealt the cards. "Cool, right? A couple of them even went on to be on Broadway! She showed me newspaper clippings about it at the library. And she has a piano at her house that she wants to show me sometime. She's been taking lessons since she was five."

"Oh, wow," I said. "I didn't know that." I wasn't exactly sure if I was referring to the Broadway people thing or the Afiya-and-the-piano thing. I guess I didn't know about either. Both facts were actually really cool. But for some reason I couldn't get myself to admit it out loud.

I threw a seven a little harder than I meant to.

She threw an eight. I played a nine.

"Oh, and it turns out I like dark chocolate best. And red jelly beans. The strawberry ones. Not cherry. And cats! Afiya showed me this video of a cat looking at itself in the mirror. It was amazing."

"Sounds great," I said.

"It was so funny. I think I really like funny videos of cats."

She added a jack to our pile.

I looked at the options in my hand, and I knew what to do right away.

Jack.

There it was, right out of my story. Exactly how I pictured it. Lots of slapping and lots of laughing. Only Zoe was laughing not really because of the hilarious slappy-ness, I didn't think, but still because she was thinking about the funny cat video, which didn't actually sound that funny.

But, then again, maybe it was. It must have been, if she thought so. And she was totally laughing about it with me.

I should probably start laughing, then.

My laughter sounded fake and it felt fake but I kept doing it. Maybe fake laughs were like fake smiles. Dad told me once that if you smiled, even if you were crabby, it could actually change your mood and eventually you'd really feel like smiling. So maybe soon enough I'd feel like laughing for real.

But I didn't.

This was supposed to be a perfect best-friend moment, but something was wrong.

"This is the best," Zoe said. I waited for the happy feeling, but it didn't come. And when Mom shouted, "Dinner!" from the kitchen—and then raced around the house shouting it some more—I hung back, waiting, thinking maybe it needed a little more time. Maybe you couldn't rush real happy feelings.

But maybe you couldn't write them into happening, either.

≈

"I'd like to make a toast," Mom said once we were sitting around the table. She held up her glass as high as she could reach. "To passing today's appointment with flying colors." Dad held up his glass, too, and Bo, Zoe, and I followed. "You've been very brave," she said to Dad, "and we're all so proud of you."

Dad smiled, but his eyes were dull, and I could tell he was counting down the minutes until dinner was over and he could go back to sleep.

"Does that mean cancer is all gone?" Bo asked.

"It seems to be all gone," Mom said. Everyone grinned, but my mouth wouldn't do it. It was like somehow it knew that it was too soon. That this was good, but not totally official.

We clinked our cups together, and I looked at Zoe. I didn't know what I was waiting for—maybe a smile or a poke in the arm like the one she'd given me last night. A poke that said *I know you don't know how to explain the way you're feeling right now, because it's this weird happy/sad/scared/excited kind of thing, but I totally understand, and I still think you're great.* But that poke and that smile didn't come.

Mom and Dad passed around plates and scooped out portions and did all those regular dinner things, and Zoe started chatting with me about other funny videos she'd watched. It was great Zoe was happy, and I was glad she was having so much fun here with me and at school and everywhere else.

I was. I really was. So the bad, annoying feeling in my gut, whatever it was, was just going to have to go away.

22
Story Problems

"Jade, can I talk to you for a second before you go to lunch?"

I went up to Mrs. Yang's desk after English on Friday. Whatever this was, I hoped it wouldn't take long. I wasn't going to try to write Zoe's every thought and every move, and I wasn't going to try to force feelings. But I had written a line in my notebook about Zoe eating with me—and only me. Problem was, if I wasn't there, she'd definitely find other people to eat with. And I probably wouldn't be too excited about who that could be.

"Thanks again for letting me take a look at some of your work," said Mrs. Yang. She handed me the copy of my story. There were bright purple marks all over it. "I finally had a chance to jot down some of my thoughts. I think it's so clever how you incorporated our new student into your story."

I bit my lip.

"A lot of writers are inspired by their friends," she continued. "It's wonderful to be able to bring elements from real life into your stories. Like I mentioned the other day, real life can be so inspiring, which is why it's important to make sure you're enjoying that too."

A giant sigh escaped my mouth. For a second I thought she was going to say something like, *It's wonderful that what you write becomes real, right?* but she hadn't. For now, the secret was safe.

"This story shows a lot of talent," she said. "Lots of smiley faces in my notes. But as far as revision goes, I'd love you to think about how you might strengthen the plot. I know I told you that it's okay to leave some things out of stories, but characters need to have layers and interact in different ways. They can't go around being happy and having fun all the time. It's okay for them to make mistakes and to try things and fail. They can have problems and disagree, like real friends sometimes do."

"Mmhmm."

There she went again, going on and on about real life. I paid attention to real life, thank you very much. And real life was exactly why I had to write so much. If I didn't, someone's real life would literally fall apart. Anyway, if Zoe and I had a problem or disagreed in a story, that would mean we would have one in real life. No way was I going to write something like that.

Mrs. Yang smiled. "Give it some thought and go back to it when you're ready. I really like the characters you've created, but try to dig deeper. Everyone has layers; everyone faces tricky situations and tough feelings. The more you explore that, the stronger your stories will be."

"Sure," I said.

I turned away from her and tried to ignore the bad feelings bubbling up inside. Mrs. Yang was a little wrong before, about how I needed to pay more attention to real life, but now she was really wrong. My stories would be fine if people stayed happy. No, not fine. Better than fine. Great. I bet she wouldn't know a good story if it walked up to her and said, *Hi, I'm awesome.*

I took a breath and went to catch up to Zoe, but she was already heading into the hall, and Clue was right on her tail. He looked like he was purposely sticking close to her. Something felt fishy, and it wasn't the fish sticks being served for lunch today.

I tapped Clue on the shoulder. Zoe kept walking, but he stayed back.

"Hi," I said. "Quick question. Are you following Zoe?"

He raised an eyebrow. "I'm not trying to. I'm just trying to figure out if there's a way I can keep her around and also have my person come to life.

"But there's not," he finished. "I tried again last night. It must just be a one-person-at-a-time kind of thing."

"Oh."

He tried to catch my eye, but my gaze darted all over the place. A million knots bounced around in my stomach, only they didn't feel like knots at all. They felt like bowling balls.

"No," I whispered, still looking away. "Please don't switch yet. I want her to be here. I need more time."

"More time to what?" Clue asked. "Brainwash her into staying your best friend? Jade, I chose you because I knew you were writing about someone you really wanted to be a part of your life. I thought you wanted a friend. But yesterday you made it seem like all you want is someone to control." Then he added, "The switch could be quick and easy."

"Please," I said. "Don't. Not yet. I . . . I can't. I'm not ready. I need time to figure things out and make them right. And then I need time to say goodbye. A *good* goodbye. You know?"

Clue made a face like someone had punched him in the guts. "Yeah," he said, "I know."

I took a breath. "Okay then. Cool."

I wanted to walk away, but something stopped me.

"Are you okay?" I asked. He looked lost in thought.

He opened his mouth but stopped his thought. "Yeah, it's nothing," he said. He looked at the floor. "Hey, do you want to work on our health project after school? I could meet you in the library."

"Um . . . I might not be able to," I said. "I'd have to check with my mom to see if she can pick up my brother . . . and I need to be home for dinner."

"I think Zoe and Afiya are working on theirs again," he added.

I blinked. "I could probably make it work."

"Cool," he said.

"Cool," I agreed.

Cool, I repeated in my head.

And I hoped with everything I had that somehow, some way, it would be.

23
The Library

I never realized how busy the library was after school. I guess it was because I was never there; I was picking up Bo or hanging out with Zoe. And before Real Zoe, I'd been writing about Fake Zoe. Anyway, the place was packed. A lot of people were reading, obviously, but some people were making art projects out of old books. Others were building something out of teeny tiny wooden pieces. Somebody else was making a movie using an iPad and a bunch of Legos.

I eyed the table by the fiction section. Zoe and Afiya were working, just like Clue said they would be. They were working all the time, it seemed like. They'd worked all through lunch, and now they were at it again. Only this time it didn't look like they were working at all. They were doing some of the fun library activities. And they weren't alone—the seats around their table were totally full, and that didn't even stop people from standing around them. I recognized people from all my different classes. Even a couple teachers were crowded around, watching what was going on.

I tore my eyes away from them and forced myself to look back at Clue. We had our whole giant table to ourselves. It was just us and a ginormous stack of books and articles about livers.

Sometimes things were really unfair.

"If you want to go say hi to your friends, I'd understand," I told Clue.

He looked over there but shook his head. "Nah, I'm good. Do you want to go say hi to Zoe?"

I ran a hand through my hair. I thought I had, but now I wasn't so sure. There was just so much going on over there. I didn't want to get in the way. "Maybe later."

Clue sighed. "Why is it so important to you that Zoe stays, anyway? Like really. I know you're a nice person. It's not about having someone to boss around. So what is it?"

I tapped my fingers on the table. "Why is it so important to you that she goes?" I asked back.

"It's not about her going. It's just what I told you: I don't think the pond water works for two people at a time. And I need someone here like you needed Zoe."

"But you have friends," I shot back. He ate lunch with different people every single day, so who could he possibly need to bring to life? Why couldn't he just let me have Zoe?

"I guess," Clue said. He gazed at the crowd by Zoe and Afiya's table. Not a single person had looked his way since we walked in.

A funny thought crossed my mind. Maybe Clue had friends—like, a lot of friends—but maybe he didn't have a best friend. Maybe none of his friends were just right for him. Was that a thing?

OPPSERVATION: People can have friends but still feel lonely.

Questions for further research: Is that why Clue wants to bring someone else to life?

I glanced at all of our study supplies.

"Let's get this over with," I said.

He handed me one of the books from the stack and I flipped through it. The dumb liver—well, a picture of one—stared back at me. The more I looked at it, the more it really didn't look like much. It was like when you stare at a certain word or write it over and over again. Soon it doesn't look like anything real. After a while the liver looked like any other piece of meat. And not too much after that, it just looked like a blob. How could something so blobby, so nothing-y, so little, cause so many big problems?

"Are you learning things?" Clue asked.

"Oh, yeah." I was definitely learning things. The liver was even dumber than I thought it was.

"You know, the liver is powerful beyond measure."

I frowned. What was that supposed to mean?

"Cool," I said, in a voice that made it clear that I didn't think it was cool at all and so maybe we could stop talking about it.

"If you ever want to talk about why the liver is important to you, you can talk about it with me," Clue added.

Okay, now he was being really weird. Did Clue know about my dad? I didn't tell him about my dad that day he wouldn't give up the window room at the hospital. And if he did know, why didn't he just come out and say so?

"Okay," I said.

I thought "thanks" in my head, but for some reason I couldn't make myself say it out loud. So I didn't.

24
Our Mission

The second I walked in the door with all the dumb liver books Clue had made me check out to read over the weekend in my arms, Mom threw my purple squishy bag at my head. It landed on the floor behind me, because what was I supposed to do, grow a third hand?

"Hi," she said. "Pack!"

"What?"

"Catch!" Bo appeared from the living room, and Mom tossed him his red bag with all the farm animals on it.

"Mom, slow down!"

She zoomed around the house faster than a person on Rollerblades. I actually checked her feet—nope, she wasn't wearing her Rollerblades at the moment, but I wouldn't be surprised if she had been. I tried to follow her, first with my feet and then with my eyes, but both ways made me dizzy.

"Can't slow down. Have to pack. Have to clean. Have to organize." She paused for a millisecond. A grin exploded on her face like a Fourth of July firework. *Bam! Kaboom!* "We're going on vacation!"

"Chemo-cation," Dad called from his chair.

"*Chemo-cation,*" she echoed. "The cancer center called. There are a few patients who've gone into remission recently—people with families, like us—and they won a grant that will pay for all of us to take a relaxing trip to the Grand Canyon together! It's last minute for us because one family canceled, and Dad is well enough to go. I don't think we can pass this up."

"A trip, a trip!" Bo jumped up and down. "I'm gonna bring Giraffe, and my papers, and my twisty crayons, and my Big Time Action Man, and the royal princesses, and all my Legos!" He rushed up the stairs, taking them two at a time, but then he came back. "Wait. What's our mission?"

"Re-mission," Dad called. "It's just a fancy way to say I'm good for now."

"For now?" Bo asked.

It was great news, but Bo looked as worried as I felt. For now was good, but it didn't mean forever. Dad could still get sick again. He could get too tired to have dinner with us like the other night. He could have a totally normal day, and then, *bam*, end up at the hospital like he did that day in fourth grade.

Bo's worried face passed. "I'm going to bring my twisty markers, too! And my goggles and my juggling balls and my Easy-Bake Oven." He raced back up the stairs.

"And clothes!" Mom shouted after him. "Bo! Clothes. Pajamas. Underwear!" she hollered. "He's going to need more bags," she said to me.

I stayed where I was and tried to smile or nod or do something to make it look like I was excited. Sure, a trip sounded amazing, but who were these other people we'd be on vacation with? And where exactly were we going, and when were we leaving? And would I have to miss school, and what about Zoe? I couldn't leave Zoe, especially not now. I'd stopped Clue from switching her out for now. But by the time I got back, Zoe could be a permanent member of the Sparkles, or worse, swapped out by Clue for someone else.

My mouth dried up but wet, sticky beads of sweat formed everywhere else. For two years I'd wanted to go on a vacation. To leave Colorado, to leave this town that everybody else got to leave all the time. And now that I could, it was the last thing on the planet I wanted to do.

"You're still standing there. Why? I need you to move. We need to move. We leave first thing in the morning! There are things that must be done!" Mom waved her feather duster in the air like a baton.

"Give her a minute, Lila." I heard Dad's voice from the living room again. "She probably has questions. C'mere, Jade."

My feet felt stuck to the ground, but I pushed them forward until they took me all the way to the living room.

Where Dad was *standing*.

Apparently Dad stood a lot during the day, but I never really saw it because I was in school. By the time I got home, he was all tired out. But there was something different right now. Right now he had real energy.

I smiled at Dad as he put an arm on my shoulder.

"What'd you and Zoe do today? Everything good with my daughters?"

I exhaled and thought about all the things I wasn't going to say. What'd we do today? Well, Zoe went to class. Spent way too much time with the Sparkles. Was the most popular person in the library and probably the whole world too. Pretty much forgot that I existed.

"Dad, it sounds like we don't have time for that. What's going on with this trip?"

He smiled and patted my head, and I stood on my tiptoes and peeked up at his. There was no hat today. Instead, there were a few springy brown-ish-grayish hairs poking out, like the first teeny flower buds blooming in spring.

"We're going to Arizona for a few days," he said. "We leave first thing in the morning tomorrow and come back Monday night." Like he could read my mind, he added, "I know it's kind of spur-of-the-moment, but we're lucky they invited us, and extremely lucky that I'm well enough to go. I'm sure your teachers will understand missing one day of school. This is a pretty big deal for our family."

It totally was a big deal, but my life at school right now was a big deal too. I couldn't leave everything and everybody, even if it meant I'd get to go on a plane and see cool places that weren't Tiveda. Missing the weekend and one day of school wasn't that much, but it was all the time Clue would need to get rid of Zoe forever if he decided to. It was more than enough time, probably. He could get rid of her and still have time to give clues and eat lunch and steal hospital rooms and study livers and do whatever else Clue did every day.

There had to be a way I could go on the trip and not have to worry about that the whole time. Maybe there was a way I could hide her or something, so Clue couldn't get her while I was gone.

Or . . .

That was it!

"Dad, I know my new friend Zoe from across the street isn't technically part of the family, but do you think I could maybe ask her to come with us? Would it cost a lot of money?"

Dad looked like he was thinking. "I'm not sure," he said.

Mom poked her head into the living room. "How's it going, people? What am I missing? Why are we not packing?"

"Jade wants to invite Zoe from across the street along," Dad said.

Mom made a face I couldn't quite read. "Sorry, sweetie," she said. "The trip is only for families. I think it'll be really good for the four of us to have some quality time together, don't you?"

"Yeah, sure, but . . ."

Mom held up a hand. "It's not up for discussion," she said.

My heart pounded. This was so unfair! Bo got to bring his friends places sometimes. Not Grand Canyon types of places, but still. I knew exactly what would happen. We would get there and Mom would start cleaning everything and Bo would want to play with his toys and Dad would be tired. And I'd be stuck by myself, thinking about all the fun Zoe was having while I was gone.

I took a deep breath and tried to get my heart to chill out a little bit. After all, we were going on vacation, and that was awesome. The more I tried to calm down, though, the more stressed out I became. I was going to be gone for three whole days. Meanwhile, Zoe would be here. With Afiya. And Clue.

And a pond full of magical water that could send her away forever.

25
Can Sir in the Sky

"Please make sure your tray tables are up and your seats are in the upright position. Flight attendants, please prepare for takeoff."

From the seat next to me, Bo stared straight ahead with a terrified look on his face. He pulled on Giraffe so hard I thought Giraffe's stuffed head might fly right off.

I understood that feeling. I mean, not exactly. It wasn't my first time on a plane. But I was so nervous about leaving Zoe that if I were holding a stuffed giraffe, I'd probably squeeze the poor thing half to death too.

I really needed to write in my notebook—something about how while I was gone, she has a lot of fun (by herself) while patiently waiting for me to get back—but I couldn't ignore my brother at a time like this. Seeing him so upset made me feel worse than I already did.

"Hey." I pried Giraffe out of his death grip and took his hand in mine. "It's going to be okay," I told him. "Flying is fun. We get to go up into the sky."

He answered immediately. "What if the bad guy is in the sky?"

"Hmm. Well, I don't think the bad guy is. But maybe you could draw a picture of the airplane defeating him."

"Why?"

"Because that might make you feel better."

Bo whimpered and shook his head. His arms shook too.

"Or maybe I could draw a picture of the airplane defeating him," I said. "And you can tell me what to do."

He bobbed his head up and down. I ripped out a page from my notebook, and we got to it.

"Okay," I said. I took my pencil and drew a long plane-shaped thing. It looked more like a hot dog than a plane, but oh, well. It was the thought that counted. "Now how exactly do I make the bad guy?" I asked.

Bo leaned in and pointed to the paper. "First you need the can. It's an oval and it's silver and you can *not* forget the crown."

I giggled to myself as I drew the thing the best I could. Bo rammed his head into my shoulder.

"That's not Can Sir," he laughed. "That's a blob with another blob on top. That's Mr. Blob Blob!"

My eyebrows squished together. "What did you just say?"

"Mr. Blob Blob," Bo repeated.

"Before that."

"You made Can Sir wrong."

I glanced behind me to see if Mom and Dad were listening, but they were both sound asleep.

"So the bad guy's name is . . . cancer?" I asked.

Bo grabbed the pencil out of my hand. "Yeah, and you make him like this," he said.

"Cancer?" I asked again.

Bo laughed. "Do you have spaghetti in your ears? I already said that." He repeated it one more time extra slowly. "Can. Sir."

I leaned back and took a slow breath. I had heard

him right. The bad guy's name was Can Sir. Can Sir. *Cancer.*

Bo *knew* about Dad's cancer? Like, really knew?

I thought about that day when Mom and Sleeping Dad had sat us down. Mom told us not to make them worry, Bo said he hoped Dad got his sorts back on, and then . . . nothing. I was scared, and apparently Bo was scared too. But I didn't do anything to help him. I didn't do anything for so long that Bo picked up his Giraffe because his own sister wasn't hugging him, and then she couldn't hug him because she was too busy hugging a notebook.

I didn't think Bo understood. But he did, in his own way. He pictured cancer like a can, with a crown. And apparently for Bo, when you called someone sir, they obviously had to wear a crown.

I leaned forward and observed our new picture. Bo had calmed way down, and now he was happily drawing away like we were hanging out at home, not sitting on an airplane thousands of feet above the ground.

I'd seen so many of these pictures. I hadn't counted, but the number had to be somewhere in the millions. But now I was seeing Bo's art in a whole new way. I was seeing *Bo* in a whole new way.

"Mr. Blob Blob is better now," he informed me.

I ruffled his hair. "Thanks. Hey, Bo?"

"Yeah, Jadey?"

"You know Can Sir is . . . defeated, right? He's not a real bad guy anymore. Dad's all better."

Bo gave me a questioning look. "Are you sure?"

"Pretty sure, yeah."

"But what if the bad guy comes back? He's very powerful, you know. He's the most powerful bad guy in this whole planet."

I swallowed hard. "Yeah, I know. I'm not sure what we do. I guess we just . . . help each other if we get scared of him." Tears poked at the corners of my eyes. I blinked them back and wrapped my arm around Bo's shoulder.

"You were really scared of him," he told me.

I laughed, even though it wasn't funny. Kindergarteners weren't just good at making friends. They were good at understanding things too. Like way better than I ever thought. Maybe little kids like Bo didn't know everything. They just knew the important things.

"Yeah," I said. "I was scared. And so were you. The whole time."

I frowned. There had been so many sad and

scary moments during Dad's treatments. Moments where I should have helped Bo. But I'd reached for Zoe instead.

OPPSERVATION: It's so obvious when you need other people. But it's easy to forget that other people need you too.

Questions for further research: Is it too late to be there for my brother the way I wished I had been before?

"But what if the bad guy comes back?" Bo asked me again. "He is big-time scary, Jade."

Now I knew the answer more than ever.

"We deal with him together," I said.

That answer seemed to calm Bo. Weirdly, it sort of calmed me too. I waited for him to ask why, but instead, he snuggled closer into my shoulder, and I rested my head on top of his.

"Want to draw more pictures?" I asked.

He snuggled even closer. "No," he said, "I just want to stay like this."

I smiled.

"Me too," I said.

26
A Big Splash

"Welcome to Arizona, folks! We're now descending and should be on the ground in the next five to ten minutes. Weather's seventy-nine degrees and sunny, with five-miles-per-hour winds from the north. The current time is 10:09 A.M. Mountain Standard Time. Thanks for flying with us today, and we hope you enjoy your stay."

The warm air washed over me the second we got off the plane. It was nice but weird too. We were really here. This was really happening. And while I was excited to spend more time with Bo, I couldn't help wondering what Zoe was up to at home.

My heart beat faster with every step we took toward baggage claim. Anything could've happened these past couple hours. By now, Zoe could be best friends with Afiya. They could've already spent the whole morning together, shopping, eating, and doing all kinds of fun things. Right this minute, Zoe could be asking herself, *So who's Jade, again?* Or worse, not asking that at all, because she was having too much fun for my name to even cross her mind.

I picked up my pace and tried to get my family to walk faster too. We really needed to hurry up and get our bags. Then we could get in the car or on the bus or whatever thing with wheels was going to take us to the hotel faster, and I could write the whole way there.

When we found the right carousel, I raced to the front.

"Oops, sorry!" I said to someone I'd bumped into.

"It's okay," he said. He turned to face me, and I froze. My eyes must've grown a zillion times their normal size.

"Clue?"

"Jade?"

"What are you doing here?" we asked at the same time.

He swayed back and forth on his sneakers.

"I'm . . . I'm on a trip," he said.

"Me too."

"Nice."

We stayed quiet after that, but my mind sure didn't. Of all the people in the world, Clue and his family were taking a trip to the same place my family was, at the same time, and they'd been on the *same flight*? It was too weird. Maybe he was on an expedition to find more magical bodies of water or something. But still—*weird*.

At least, if Clue was here, that meant he wasn't in Tiveda. And if he wasn't in Tiveda, he couldn't go ahead and swap Zoe out for his person while I was gone.

Maybe she was doing things I wasn't so sure about, but at least she was safe.

I spotted our bags and called for Mom to come help. Once we'd gathered them, I turned back to Clue.

"Well, have a good trip," I told him.

He smiled. "You too."

And now that Zoe was safe—and that I'd finally have some time to write—I knew that I would.

≈

Zoe and Jade were apart, and Zoe was not happy.

She paced back and forth across her house (that had all the furniture she needed to be comfortable and happy). "I wonder what Jade is doing right now," she wondered out loud. Sadly no one answered.

Zoe knew she needed to think of something to do while Jade was gone. Otherwise she'd be really, really bored.

"Maybe I could make a list of ideas," Zoe thought. So she grabbed some paper she found in her house and got to work.

Play games.

Watch movies.

Read.

Repeat.

Zoe smiled to herself. There! It wasn't a long list of activities, but it was enough to make it until Monday night. Games like Solitaire could be played over and over again. Movies were long, and there were millions of them to choose from. Same with books. Mrs. Yang always said you could never read enough books. You could even read the same books over and over again, because maybe you'd discover something you hadn't noticed your first time through. Even though Mrs. Yang's advice had been wrong lately, that idea was right.

Mom interrupted my writing. "Jade, look!" she said. "Mountains! Aren't they beautiful?"

"Yay," I said, but I didn't look up. I couldn't waste time. (And we had mountains in Colorado, anyway.)

Zoe was excited. It'd be a good weekend. And when Jade got back on Monday night, they'd tell each other everything they did, and they'd jump right back into their friendship like no time had passed at all.

"Look," Mom called again. Bo and Dad *ooh-ed* and *ahh-ed*, but I ignored them and looked over what I'd written. It wasn't my best work, but it would have to do for now. Maybe once we got to the hotel, I'd give Zoe a call and make sure she had ideas. Anyway, I was trying to trust her at least a little. I hadn't told her what to read or watch. There were plenty of blanks she could fill in on her own.

I sat back and squeezed Bo's hand. Now that I was sure everything would be fine, I could finally relax and enjoy the trip. I got ready to *ooh* and *ahh* at the next mountain, but I guess I was too late, because nobody made any more happy noises the whole rest of the drive. But whatever. Once I talked to Zoe and made sure everything was good, I could make some happy noises of my own.

≈

We didn't have any official trip activities until lunchtime, so I asked Mom if I could borrow her phone and go to the hotel pool. When I got there, I dipped my toes in the water, took a deep breath, and gave my best friend a call on her home phone.

She answered right away. "That was fast!" she said.

"Huh?"

"Who is this?"

"Jade?"

"Oh," Zoe giggled. "Sorry. I thought it was Afiya. We were just talking and she said she'd call me right back. But that was literally a second ago. She wouldn't have called back that fast. Funny, right?"

"Yeah," I agreed.

I cleared my throat. "I wanted to make sure you weren't too bored without me."

"Aw, that's so nice! Don't worry about me. I'm totally fine. Afiya and I were actually just making plans. We're going to have a sleepover tonight at her house with Camilla and Maggie. Afiya says we can play games, watch movies, and take some magazine quizzes." Zoe took her first breath in what felt like a very long time. "We'll miss you, of course," she added, "but it's going to be so fun!"

I pushed my feet into the water and kicked them up and down, up and down, up and down. Water splashed into the air with each satisfying smack.

"Jade? Are you there?"

"I . . ."

"Oh, you know what? That's actually Afiya calling me back. I have to go, okay? Have an awesome time on your trip. Can't wait to see you when you get back!"

"Yeah, I . . ."

I didn't have time to finish my sentence. Zoe had already hung up.

I kicked my legs harder and harder. Most of my body wasn't even in the pool, but it felt like I'd done the biggest belly flop of all time. That was *not* how the call was supposed to go. Not. At. All.

I'd given her such good activities! But she'd decided on her own that if she couldn't do them with me, she'd go do them with somebody else. At a sleepover. A *sleepover*!

The belly-flop feeling got worse—right as a whole ton of water splashed onto my face.

"Hey!" I called out, wiping off my glasses.

A face emerged from the water.

No. No way. It couldn't be. And yet it totally was.

"Sorry," said Clue. "My cannonballs go wide sometimes."

"Hey, Greshie! Cannonball!" a little girl jumped off the edge, and two men on lounge chairs on the other side of the pool clapped and cheered.

"What are *you* doing here?" I asked.

Clue pushed some wet hair out of his face.

"I'm just . . . here," he said after a minute. Even with all the different feelings floating around inside of me like loose pool toys, I couldn't help but laugh.

"That was a terrible answer," I said. I kicked my legs some more. "Are you . . . are you on the trip through the cancer center?"

Clue let out a long breath. "Yeah. I am. I thought you might be on this trip, too, when I saw you at the airport," he added, "but I didn't know for sure. I guess I could have said something."

We didn't say anything for a bit. Clearly neither of us really wanted to talk about why we were on a trip like this one, or ask the other too much about it.

"You splashed me, you know," I finally told him.

"Sorry about that."

"It's okay."

"Do you want to splash me back?" he asked.

Our eyes locked. There was a funny look on his face, like he was giving me a dare but didn't think I'd really do it. I usually wasn't a very splashy person. But after my phone chat with Zoe, smacking the water didn't sound so bad. I tossed Mom's cell onto a lounge chair nearby.

Then, before Clue even realized what was happening, I leaned over, slipped my hands into the pool, and pushed as much water up and out as I possibly could.

He coughed a couple times, but the coughs quickly turned to laughs.

"Jade Levy!" he said.

"Clue Gorham," I replied.

He gave me a funny look, and I put my hands back into the water and braced myself for what I knew was coming next.

"Splash fight," he yelled.

"Unfair advantage," I called as I tried to defend myself. "You're actually in the pool!"

"Too bad, so sad," he answered.

I squealed as more water hit me and shrieked as I sent some flying back toward him.

Before I knew it, I was completely soaked from

head to toe. Which normally wouldn't be that big of a deal, but there was the tiny fact that I was still in my shorts and T-shirt.

"Here, let me help you with that," Clue said. He got out of the pool and tossed a big handful of towels at my head.

"Oh, you're so kind," I said as I tossed towels back on him. "Let me help you too. It's only fair."

Clue grinned. "Towel fight?"

I was laughing so hard I could barely answer.

When Mom came down to tell me it was time to go to lunch, she was a little bit confused. We had moved on to seeing how many towels we could stack on each other's heads before they fell over. So far I had six, and Clue trailed behind with four.

Mom took her phone back and snapped a picture.

"I have no idea what's happening here, but I absolutely support it," she said. We laughed at that, which made us wobble, which—

"Ahhh!"

"Take cover!"

—made all the towels fall down.

"How was your chat with Zoe?" Mom asked as we picked them up and got in the elevator to go up to our room.

I shrugged. "Okay."

For a second I'd totally forgotten how stressed I was after that call.

And even though it was on my mind now, as I changed into dry clothes, I couldn't stop smiling.

27
Getting a Clue

After I changed we met everyone in our cancer-center group in the hotel lobby.

There was Clue, his dads, and the little girl from the pool, who must be his little sister. There were two other families, also—one with a mom and two little boys, and another one with a mom, a dad, and four little kids who looked even younger than Bo. I beamed at my brother, remembering the flight here.

Clue and I waved at each other as the leader of the trip, a cute old guy named Ray, made sure we were all accounted for.

"Sixteen, seventeen, eighteen," he finished, and marked something on his clipboard. "All right, folks. Let's get this started. Hop on the bus for a tour and picnic lunch extravaganza!"

My thoughts turned to Zoe as we went outside and boarded the giant bus. Our call was so weird. Why was it that the more I tried to make things perfect between us, the more complicated they got? My stomach flip-flopped just thinking about it.

Bo wanted to sit with Clue's sister, so I took a window seat in the row across from him and flipped my notebook open as everyone else got on.

Zoe was making more and more of her own choices, and Jade couldn't help it—she was freaking out. Zoe was doing the activities Jade wrote about, but instead of doing them on her own, she'd decided to go do them at a sleepover with practically every girl in their entire school. Which was fine. Right? It was fine. Jade was trying to trust Zoe. And even though it would've made Jade feel better if Zoe decided to be alone, she had to believe that Zoe could have fun with other people while still remembering that her best friend was Jade.

She had to believe it. Had to.

But what if she couldn't?

"Working on a new Zoe story?" Clue interrupted.

"How long have you been sitting there?"

Clue shrugged. "Long enough to figure out what you're up to."

I jerked my head toward the green notebook in his lap. "What are you up to? Remembering the time you lost a splash fight against somebody who wasn't even in the pool?"

"Yeah, pretty sure *lose* doesn't mean what you think it means. I was undeniably the winner."

"Sure," I said. "Go ahead and think that. Whatever makes you feel better."

Clue laughed.

"For real, though," he said. "What are you writing?"

"Just . . . trying to figure out some Zoe stuff," I said. "You?" I squirmed in my seat.

He eyed his notebook. "Working on a story."

"About what?"

"My sister."

"Oh," I said. "Harper or Fallan?"

Fallan, who was probably four, had become fast friends with Bo. They had some super-detailed princess-and-Giraffe-rescue-the-Legos-game going on in the row across from us.

Harper was the one he'd mentioned before, the one who had all the theories about things. The one who believed the pond was magical.

But Harper wasn't here.

Suddenly I was piecing it all together. It all made sense. Why Clue was at the cancer center that day. Why he was on this trip now. Clue didn't say anything else. He didn't have to. Deep down, somehow, I just knew.

"So Harper . . ." I started.

"Had cancer," Clue finished. "Yeah. When she was in sixth grade and I was in fourth. She had a tumor in her brain. And then she died."

I sank into my seat as a guilty feeling spread through me. I was always kind of bummed about Dad, but maybe I should spend more time appreciating that he was doing okay.

"My sister loved to travel," Clue said, and I sat up to hear him. "This trip seemed like a good way to honor her."

I bit my lip. "So a couple years ago, when I saw you at the cancer center, you were there for her?"

"That was after she passed away," he said. "We liked to go back and visit her doctors and nurses. Still do. I was visiting her old room that day."

I leaned my head against the window and took a few breaths. I had assumed the worst about Clue that day. And about my own problems and Dad's.

I glanced at his notebook again. "Do you write about her a lot?"

He sighed. "All the time. She . . . she was my best friend. I mean, I love my little sister too, but my dads adopted Harper and me together. Before they came along, it was just the two of us." He cleared his throat. "So I guess you know what I'm really trying to do, huh?"

I bit my lip and looked away. Who was I to want to keep my imaginary best friend when he wanted to see his big sister?

I looked back. "Just wondering . . . why did you bring Zoe here if you really wanted to bring your sister?"

Now it was Clue's turn to squirm in his seat. "I just wanted to see if everything worked okay. See what it'd be like if someone actually did come to life. Ever since you told me about your Zoe notebook at the cancer center, I've been curious about it. I've been observing you at school. Not in a creepy way."

We both laughed quietly.

"Sure," I said. "Just in a want-to-see-if-your-character-would-make-a-good-real-person way."

"Yeah," Clue agreed.

He seemed like he wanted to say more, but he looked at his notebook instead. A weird taste flooded my mouth even though I hadn't eaten anything since the plane. I definitely felt bad for Clue, but at the same time, it was weird that he'd used Zoe and me to test out his plan. It was like my whole friendship with her was practice for something that didn't actually involve us at all.

"These are our real lives, though," I told him. "Zoe's and mine. We're not experiments. We're people."

Clue frowned. "I know," he said, "but I *need* Harper. If Zoe goes, you can write about her again, like before. She's real but she's not, not really."

I frowned too. "She's real to me, though. She's my best friend."

Clue didn't say anything, but the look on his face showed that he didn't understand, didn't think Zoe was nearly as important as his sister. And she wasn't, I guess. Nothing could be worse than losing someone you loved. Still, Zoe was important to me. And Clue was acting like that didn't matter.

I turned away. I crossed my legs, then uncrossed them, then crossed them again. I didn't want to say anything mean and make things worse. But I couldn't think of anything nice to say, either.

So I didn't say anything at all.

28
The Plan

I didn't know when we were getting to the lunch portion of this bus ride, but it was starting to seem like never.

Or maybe it just seemed like never because Clue and I hadn't said a word to each other in what felt like hours, but we were still stuck being seatmates.

"Bringing Zoe here wasn't *only* because I wanted to test out the magic, you know," he finally said.

I turned to face him.

"It wasn't?"

"No," he said. "You might not want to believe it, but I'm not actually a jerk."

I cracked a small smile. "I know you're not. So why *did* you bring her here?"

Clue shrugged. "I kept an eye on you, like I said. And from what I noticed, you seemed like you could use a friend," he said in a quiet voice. "You still seem that way."

I raised my eyebrows. "So you're saying Zoe's not a good friend?"

"I'm not saying that," he said. "But maybe you shouldn't care if your best friend has other friends."

"So you're saying *I'm* not a good friend."

"I'm not saying that either! I'm just saying . . . maybe your friendship isn't what you think it is."

I folded my arms across my chest. That wasn't true.

Except maybe it was. The truth was, I stressed about my best-friendship all the time.

"It wasn't like that with Harper?" I asked.

Clue shook his head as the bus rolled to a stop. "Nah," he said. "I mean, she had a ton of friends. But she and I were the ultimate friends, even for being siblings. We could talk about everything, like her tumor. Or laugh about anything, like our Pop's bad sense of direction, even with a GPS. Once we were trying to go to that one fancy grocery store in Denver and we ended up in Wyoming."

I giggled as Ray announced it was time for lunch. "Everybody off!" he called. "We've got egg salad and tuna salad. Please think about what you want as you exit the vehicle so we can hand out sandwiches quickly and efficiently."

Clue scooted out and made room for me to stand in the aisle. As I waited my turn to get off, I had a lot to think about. Sandwiches were only the beginning.

≈

"Okay, Clue."

I went up to him after we ate and before I lost my nerve. The egg salad churned around in my stomach.

"Okay what?"

"Okay, you can make the switch. Zoe's important to me, but she's not my sister. We're not as close as you and Harper were."

I couldn't believe what I was saying, but there I was, saying it.

"No," he said.

I raised my eyebrows. "What?"

He took a gulp of water. "What if there was a way we could have them both?"

Heat rose to my cheeks. "I thought you said that wouldn't work."

Clue stood up. "I never actually tried it."

My pulse raced. "You said you did. *Twice*."

"Well, I didn't," he snapped. Then quietly, he added, "I was too chicken." He started walking toward a small woodsy area near the picnic tables. "Come on," he called.

My heart thudded. There was no time to worry or wonder or wish. I just had to trust him, even though he was obviously upset about something.

"Wait up," I called.

Of course Bo and Fallan had to follow us.

"Sorry," I whispered to Clue. "I didn't mean to get us stuck babysitting."

He gazed at his little sister. "It's cool. I like being near her."

"Yeah, me too," I said as I watched Bo.

Clue turned back to me, all business.

"Okay," he said. "So here's my idea. I used three drops of pond water to bring Zoe to life. I'm wondering if maybe I need to use more drops on Harper, since she was a real person."

I nodded. "Yeah. Plus, I only have two years of Zoe stories. You have way more than that about Harper, right?"

"Uh-huh. So maybe I do what I did to your notebook, but I double the amount of drops."

"Or even triple or quadruple," I added, "just to be sure."

"And if I leave your notebook out entirely, it shouldn't impact Zoe."

"But, um, Clue. One little thing. We're in Arizona. There's no magical Tiveda pond here."

"That's why I brought this!" Clue pulled a tube out of his backpack like he was a magician pulling a rabbit out of a hat. It seemed like a lot of magicians got that wrong, but Clue knew exactly what he was doing. The tube was the same one I'd seen him use at the pond, and sure enough, it was full of murky, bubbly, awesome water.

"Amazing," I said.

He took a loud breath. "You know what they say—never leave home without a tube of magical water."

I laughed. "Do they say that?"

"I say that," he said with a smile. Clue hadn't taken his eyes off the tube of water.

I watched it too. "So you think Harper makes the magic happen?"

He thought for a minute.

"I think the pond is magical," he said, "like she always believed. It just needed a little extra help from her." He stood up straighter. "She'll make it happen now."

Clue slowly opened the tube and tipped it toward his notebook. Even with the kids playing nearby, all I could hear was my heartbeat, which seemed louder than ever.

"Here we go," Clue said. He mumbled some words while staring at the tube of water, steadying himself to pour drops of it onto his notebook. His concentration was intense. I couldn't look away.

Suddenly, Bo and Fallan appeared right beside us.

"We made a picture!" Fallan announced. Bo waved it in our faces.

Clue jumped and dropped the tube and the notebook. The water—all the water—flew out and splattered, soaking the cover of the notebook and probably some of the pages inside. It was more than double the drops that went on mine. More than triple. More than quadruple.

For a second everything was quiet. It was like all four of us were taking a collective breath and holding it tight, afraid of what might happen if we let it go.

29
The Crying Game

I squeezed my eyes closed as hard as I could.

When I opened my eyes, nothing had changed. The water had spilled, big time, and it wasn't the only water around, either. Tears streamed down Clue's face. There was no Harper in sight.

I put a hand on Clue's shoulder. "You know what they say," I joked, trying to lighten the mood. "Don't cry over spilled water."

He didn't laugh or ask *Do they say that?* or anything. He just flipped through the pages and looked around as his eyes filled all over again.

"We'll be home in a couple days," I said. "We can get more water and try again then." My voice came out quiet and not very convincing. I knew how a couple of days could feel like forever.

Tears formed in my eyes, too, but I couldn't cry. Not right now. Bo and Fallan were watching us.

OPPSERVATION: Sometimes you feel a thousand
  kinds of horrible and you have no idea what to do,
  but you have to pretend to be tough because a
  couple little kids are depending on you. And then
  you actually feel sort of tough.

Questions for further research: Am I tough for real?

I cleared my throat. "Don't worry," I told them. "Clue is just playing . . . um . . . the crying game."

"What's the crying game?" Fallan asked.

"Well, the crying game is . . . um . . . a game . . . where you pretend to cry."

Okay, this was not going well. But when I glanced at Clue out of the corner of my eye, he was . . . was he actually? Yes! He was *laughing* through his tears.

He raised an eyebrow at me and mouthed *the crying game? Really?* And then he burst out laughing again. And so did I.

I turned back to the kids. "I confess," I told them. "Clue was not playing a game. He was sad. It's okay to be sad."

Bo and Fallan nodded. Then they gave Clue big hugs and went back to playing.

I sat down next to him. "You okay?" I asked.

He exhaled. "Yeah. No. I don't know. That's why I didn't try it before, for real," he added. "That's why I made Zoe come to life first. I was stalling. I mean, I wanted to give you a friend. But I was also scared that it wouldn't work with Harper." He stared up at the sky and blinked a bunch of times.

"Sorry it got messed up," I said.

Clue rubbed a hand along the top of his head. "What am I going to do now?" he asked, more to himself than to me. "It feels like . . . I don't know. It feels like it's not meant to be."

"We'll come up with something else," I told him.

Clue wiped away the last of his tears and took a breath. "Thanks, Jade. You're a good friend."

My heart swelled. Even though things had gone wrong, there was something really nice about being called a good friend. And all I had to do was be there for Clue when things were tough.

I'd never written a story where things weren't

fun for Zoe and me. I always glossed over things about my dad. I never once wrote a story where I really listened to Zoe or felt sad for her like I was feeling with Clue.

Maybe Mrs. Yang was right after all. Real life was great inspiration for stories. But what I was writing . . . it wasn't really true to life at all. None of those situations felt as meaningful as this one did, right now. And by getting so caught up in Zoe, I'd missed out on a lot of other things going on in real life. Like the stuff with Bo. And the chance to have a real friendship with someone who'd always been right in front of my face.

My mouth twisted in a smile. Mrs. Yang always said that sometimes writers get ideas when they're out living life, when they're not even trying to think of things. And sure enough, I had.

Maybe it was finally time to revise.

30
Spiky Love

Once Clue's tears had dried, we decided to head back to our parents.

When we turned at a big tree, we could see all the adults huddled around a small campfire, roasting marshmallows and chatting in quiet voices. Of course that all changed when they saw us. If you ever want to feel popular, spend a half hour away from your parents, then come back.

"Hey!" Mom stood up and wrapped Bo and me in a big hug. Dad waved with both of his arms and grinned with his entire mouth.

Suddenly I felt totally exhausted.

I fell into Mom's arm. "Hi."

"We have a little more time before we head back to the hotel," she said. "Dad and I were thinking the four of us would go do some exploring on our own. Sound good?"

I nodded. I wanted to revise, but my stories would still be there after we walked around.

"That sounds great," I said.

Mom jumped up. "Excellent. What should we do? Anyone have ideas?"

Dad yawned. "I don't know. I think it's pretty boring here," he said. "Maybe we should go to my doctor's office. Now that's where the party is."

I groaned. "Dad. Be serious."

He made a pretend-offended face. "I am always serious."

That made us giggle more. Even though Clue's and my failed experiment was still fresh in my mind, it didn't seem quite as horrible as Mom, Dad, Bo, and I got up and made our way to a gravelly walking trail near the picnic spot.

Dad grabbed a couple pieces of grass from the side of the path and handed them to Mom. "For you, my love."

Mom used them to fan herself. "Isn't he romantic?" she asked us.

"Aww," said Bo.

"Eww," I said.

But okay. Maybe, secretly, I thought it was pretty cute.

"You think that's romantic," Dad said, "check this out. I'm going to get you your own brand-new cactus."

He bent down and pretended like he was going to pick one up.

"Dad!" Bo cried. "Those are not for picking. They are spiky, spiky, spiky!"

Dad leaned over further. "Sometimes love is spiky, bud."

Mom laughed and pulled Dad back up. "Okay, Mr. Romantic, I think that's enough."

Bo kept watching the cactus. "I want spiky love."

Mom and Dad raised their eyebrows at each other. Then they both rushed at Bo, fingernails first.

"Spiky love!" Mom shouted as she and Dad gently poked him with their nails. Bo squealed and held up his own tiny ones.

"Spiky love strikes back," he shouted, and lunged at our parents.

"Jade's turn," Mom announced.

I whipped around. "My turn for wha . . . ah!"

I squealed as the three of them hurtled toward me with their nails out. Bo grabbed my leg and Mom held me by the shoulders as Dad gently poked my arms. It was weird! It was the best! I was dizzy with feelings. And I guess I was real dizzy, too, because I wobbled left and right. I grabbed onto Bo, who grabbed onto Mom, who grabbed onto Dad, and before I knew it, all four of us were tangled in the grass, a big pile of arms and legs and fingernails and smiles.

"You're fun when you play with us, Jade," Bo said.

I smiled to myself. It always seemed that they weren't that into hanging out with me. Dad was always sitting and Mom was always moving around and Bo was always drawing. But it turned out they were doing stuff together at the same time. I thought about my walk to the pond. When I'd gotten home there was that note about Mom and Bo being out for ice cream. Or how Bo sat with Dad downstairs while I wrote about Zoe up in our room, all by myself. All this time I'd been missing out.

When we'd all caught our breath, Dad said, "Not quite as fun as a trip to the doctor, but I'll take it."

Mom elbowed him gently in the guts. "This

would make a good story, Jade," she said. "You should write about it. Or Bo, you could make a picture. The Levy family takes on the bad guy with the power of spiky love."

We all laughed except for Bo, who looked very serious. "No," he said. "I don't need to. Jade said Can Sir is defeated."

Mom and Dad sat up straight.

"What did you say?" Mom asked. I could hear the realization in her voice.

"I said, Can Sir is really defeated!"

Mom's eyes went huge, the same way mine did when Bo finally told me his bad guy's name.

"Bo, buddy," Dad said, "you and Jade are right. Cancer is defeated. We're lucky, because it's going away from us for now. It doesn't go away from everybody, but it's finally leaving us alone, hopefully for a long, long time. Maybe even forever."

Bo's eyebrows furrowed together. "We should make sure he stays defeated for good," he decided. "We should rip him up."

"Yeah, maybe we should." Dad's face was all business. "Come on," he turned to Mom and me.

The four of us walked back to the picnic area.

"Can I borrow a picture, bud?" Dad asked. Bo

grabbed the one he and Fallan had tried to show Clue and me before. It was a picture of all of us—my family, Clue's family, the other families—smiling all together, while Can Sir stood off to the side, small and alone. Carefully Dad ripped off the corner with Can Sir. Then he handed it to Mom. She ripped the crown into tiny pieces and tossed them into the fire. Then Bo took a turn, and so did I. Dad took care of the rest, and soon the corner of the paper was no more. There was nothing left.

Bo danced in a circle. "We defeated you, Can Sir," he shouted.

The words played over and over in my head.

We defeated you, cancer.

We defeated you.

Can Sir was finally gone.

31

You Choose

The next day we drove around on the bus for a while longer, before we were back at the hotel and had time to do whatever we wanted.

And what I wanted to do, surprisingly, was work on my liver project with Clue.

We spread all our stuff out at a picnic table near the hotel. There was so much information. Like, more than I could ever imagine.

I guess it was lucky I didn't have to figure it all out myself.

"I hope you don't mind studying this," he said quietly. "I didn't mean to push you so hard about it. I just thought it might help. I knew your dad had some kind of cancer. I figured it out when Mr. Kremen was all concerned about you during the class about livers."

I flipped through some pages of the book in front of me. I was expecting all the liver stuff to freak me out or make me mad. At first it had, but right now it wasn't doing that at all. It was actually making me feel sort of . . . calm. And weirdly powerful. Sure, the liver was the boss of a lot more than a little blobby thing should be, but it didn't get to determine everything. I wouldn't let it. Not anymore.

"No, it's okay," I told him. "I think this was a good idea."

I jotted down some notes and let the sun wash over me.

"You doing okay?" I asked him.

He nodded. "I think so. Thanks for checking."

I took some more notes. I had no idea the liver weighed around three pounds. That was massive! No wonder Dad's made him feel so bad.

I smiled up at Clue between notes. I always thought friends just went along with things. That they kept life simple and easy for each other. But it was cool of Clue to push for this project. Now I was figuring out why Dad needed a good, strong liver in the first place. Even though understanding the liver didn't make Dad's disease go away, something about learning this stuff made me feel a lot better.

I snuck a glance at Clue across the table. He looked back at me and smiled.

"Hey, Clue," I said. It was going to be a hard question, but I forced myself to ask it anyway. "You said Harper had a brain tumor, right?"

"Yeah," he said.

"Maybe next time we can work on a project about that."

Slowly, Clue nodded. "Maybe we can," he said.

≈

"I think I really messed up," I told Clue by the pool when we took a break from our project a little later.

"Yeah," he agreed. "You're actually wearing a bathing suit to the pool. Makes it way less fun to soak you."

I rolled my eyes. "I'm serious."

"So am I."

I gave him a little splash. Then he lifted himself out of the pool and sat beside me along the edge.

"What's up?"

"It's Zoe. I think I've been a really bad friend."

"What do you mean?"

"The whole time she's been alive, I've been so worried about losing her that I've tried to control everything. And it's been fine, I guess, sort of. But it's not real. She's been who I wanted her to be, but I have no idea who she actually is. And I never even wrote about her family. Or my family! I never wrote about us having tough conversations or being upset or anything that's actually interesting or important." Mrs. Yang's advice about characters with layers swirled in my head. "I didn't even give her a family!" I cried out.

I watched everybody else. The little kids were playing Marco Polo, and my parents were on lounge chairs, looking at each other all lovey-dovey and gross and adorable. How could I have just not tried to give Zoe parents of her own? Maybe a little brother or sister? And how could she have been so selfless not to even ask?

Clue scratched his head. "Well, she's probably had a chance to figure out who she is this weekend, right? Because you haven't had as much time to write."

"True."

Clue pointed to my mom. Her phone sat on the table next to her chair. "Only one way to find out."

I took a huge gulp of steamy Arizona air.

"You're right."

I jumped up and walked over to Mom. My heart pounded through my bathing suit. I glanced back at Clue over my shoulder, and he nodded. I could do this. I had to.

I asked Mom to use the phone. Then I walked away from everybody and found my own spot as I dialed the number and listened to it ring.

"Jade!"

She answered right away, and I let out the breath I'd been holding since I decided to give her a call.

I meant to say something like *hi*, but different words came out instead.

"I'm sorry," I said. "Zoe, I'm so, so, so sorry!"

The rest of what I'd been thinking about on the trip poured out of me like a word-waterfall. "All this time, I've been trying to make you do what I wanted and to stop you from having opinions and ideas and other friends. It wasn't very fair of me to not think about how lonely you must have been without a family. I've been such a bad friend."

There was a long pause on the other line.

"Jade, it's okay," Zoe finally said. "You were just trying to stay best friends."

"I know," I said. "I just wanted . . ."

I bit my lip. What *did* I want? At first I wanted Zoe to be around all the time, to do fun things with me and listen to me and be my best friend always and forever no matter what. But now I wanted a different kind of friend. And maybe what I wanted most of all . . . was for her to be happy. Even if that meant that things might change.

"So how was the sleepover?" I asked. "For real. I really want to know."

I listened to her go on about how they had a dance party and at first it was fun but then it made her neck too hot even if her hair was in a ponytail and how she loved spending time with new people and how they'd gone into Denver and had Chinese food and egg rolls were the best thing she'd ever eaten in her life. Then I took a slow, deep breath. A smile spread from my mouth to my cheeks to my ears. Zoe sounded different today than she ever had before. Different because she was talking about things I didn't already know about—things I hadn't made up for her.

We talked and talked and talked. About all kinds of things. Zoe had so many interesting thoughts, questions, and observations. She'd gone for a walk and stumbled across the pond. "That place is creepy!" she said. She'd also gone back to the mall, this time with Afiya. And tried out her piano. They'd even played a duet.

A little while later, Mom waved her arms at me from across the pool. "We have to go," she mouthed. "Lunch!"

"I have to go," I told Zoe.

"Aw," she said, "okay. Hey, what do you think I should do until you get back? Any ideas?"

I tipped my head back and smiled. I felt warm everywhere, and I had a hunch it wasn't just because we were in Arizona.

"Yeah, I have ideas, but so do you. You choose, Zoe."

32
The Hike

After lunch it was time for a mini hike. We were going to walk from the Visitors Center to Yavapai Point, which was supposed to be one of the very best Canyon views. Even though the walk was only a mile, Dad and the other people in remission were going to take a private shuttle. They were all healthy now, but they were still supposed to take it easy.

"We'll race you there," Bo told Dad.

"Sure thing, buddy. I bet it'll be close."

Bo giggled and grabbed my hand. I grabbed Mom's, and together we walked on the gravel path along the Canyon's rim. Clue and his family were right behind.

"Don't forget to enjoy the view," Mom reminded us as the path curved around. I looked out into the canyon, but only a little. I mostly kept my gaze fixed on her and Bo and their happy faces. That was the only view I needed.

"We're almost there," Mom said after a few minutes had passed. "Let's hurry and beat Dad!"

Bo tugged at my arm. "Go faster, Jade!"

I laughed. "I don't think I can go as fast as you."

"Why?"

"Because you're *so* fast!"

He grinned. "True."

"Hey." I wriggled my hand out of his grasp. I let go of Mom's on my other side. Then I clasped the two of them together. "You guys go ahead," I said.

For the first time in a couple days, my arms were totally free. I wasn't holding on to Bo or Zoe or Clue—or what I wanted to have happen.

Now I really looked out at the canyon. I wasn't much of an *OMG, scenery!* person. But Mom was right—it was pretty great. I usually ignored the things Mrs. Yang said about setting in stories because I thought the characters were way more important. But standing here, feeling the breeze at my back, listening to the peaceful sounds of all the nature, I realized: setting had a ton to do with character. If Zoe could go anywhere in the world, where would she go? What would she do? How would those adventures help her grow and change?

I snapped out of my thoughts when I realized I'd made it to the lookout point. I held onto the railing, peeked over the edge, and, *wow*, I had to admit: That was a view. The rocks went on forever.

The shuttle got there before we did, obviously. I saw Dad's new, barely-there curly hairs glimmering in the sunlight before I even saw him. He looked up, a huge smile on his face, like the world was wide open and he could do anything. From far away he didn't look like Sick Dad. He looked like a superhero.

But then, just like that, he *did* look like Sick Dad.

OPPSERVATION: Doctors can be wrong.

Questions for further research: Why did they have to be wrong about Dad?

It didn't make any sense. One second he was standing, happily checking out the view. And then he was on the ground, crumpled up in a ball. Everyone rushed to his side, but Ray told us to get back.

"Give him some space," he told us.

My feet froze to the ground. The whole world spun faster and faster and faster, like all it wanted was to push me over and knock me all the way down.

There aren't any opposites when something is wrong with someone you love. Or maybe there are. But there isn't time to think about them, or your questions for further research. You know that things are bad, and that's it. And when a nice old guy named Ray tells you, and only you, to run, not walk, to the Geology Center nearby to meet the ambulance, you don't think about all the zillions of things that could go wrong, you don't hear the loud pounding in your heart—you just do it. You turn and go without waving or looking back.

I darted around the trail moving faster than I've ever moved in my entire life, swerving around people left and right, paying attention to my footing on the path and the crunching of the gravel beneath my feet. My legs burned, but I took one step and another step and another step, and somehow I didn't fall.

There wasn't much wind but it was in my face. I was frozen with fear and sticky with sweat. Time went slowly and way too fast. Everything I shot past was a blur, but I noticed every person, every rock, every everything. My whole world was an opposite. It didn't make any sense. When I reached the lot at the Geology Center, I waved my arms at the ambulance people, told them where the group was, and stepped aside as they raced past me to save my dad. And as I watched them go, I hoped and wished and somehow, deep down, really believed that in some weird, not-making-any-sense kind of way, everything was going to be all right.

≈

It seemed like only a matter of seconds before the ambulance workers returned, carrying Dad on a stretcher. He looked like a big Dad-shaped lump. I swallowed hard. Even though I'd gotten here pretty quickly, maybe I had been too slow to get help, and now it was too late. Maybe they couldn't save Dad after all. But then I heard his voice.

"Hey, Jadey. I'm okay. Just tired. I really shouldn't have done those ten laps up and down the canyon before everyone woke up this morning."

I was too worried to groan at his joke. Mom squeezed my hand. I hadn't even noticed that the rest of the group had made their way over. "He's going to be fine," she said. "They think his hemoglobin probably dropped pretty low. They'll make sure everything gets back to where it needs to be." She paused, keeping her eyes on me. "Dad did way too much hiking. He's too outdoorsy for his own good." She winked. He hadn't really done any hiking at all. How could she be so calm and funny in a moment like this? Dad was on a stretcher. He wasn't better at all. He was worse.

But somehow she and Dad were still making us laugh.

There was something so not funny about how Dad had been really careful to take it easy and everything, and still, here he was on a stretcher. Talk about an Oppservation.

I leaned into Mom. "You know how Bo would draw low hemoglobin?" I asked.

"How?" Bo popped out from behind me.

"Well, I don't really know what hemoglobin means, but I can totally imagine you making a super-creepy green-goblin type of guy."

Mom and Dad laughed, and Bo grinned. "That's an amazing idea," he said. "And maybe he could pound his chest with his big, creepy, green-goblin fists, and he can yell, *He-mo-glo-bin! He-mo-glo-bin!*"

Dad laughed again, then coughed, then laughed one more time. "I'm going to run an errand really quick," he said, "but you guys keep thinking about this and let me know how it pans out." He pointed at Bo. "I expect pictures." Then at me. "And stories."

We both nodded as Dad was loaded into the ambulance.

"It's going to be okay," Clue whispered to me as Mom helped Bo inside.

I nodded as I stepped in next. "Thanks."

As the ambulance drove away, I looked out the back window and waved to all our trip friends, mostly to Clue. And even though this was scary, I kind of felt, well, lucky. It sounded like Dad was going to be fine. Mom and Bo were here with me. I had gotten help for Dad all by myself, and I had succeeded.

I squeezed Mom's and Bo's hands. Now I had a really solid idea of what I needed to write, but I wasn't going to do it right now. Now I was just going to be with them, hold them close, and try to be brave as we looked out the window and watched the world go by.

33
A New Chapter

Once we got to the hospital, Dad was taken away really fast to go have a blood transfusion. Apparently hemoglobin had something to do with blood being tired and not working right, so Dad needed to go trade his in for some blood that was more awake. "Some coffee-flavored blood," he joked as they rolled him away.

I'd been to the cancer center and other doctor-y places with Dad a bunch of times over the past couple years, but I hadn't been to an official hospital since the day of Nessa's party. This was a different hospital, obviously, but a lot of things were the same. The white walls. The long, endless hallways. The way everybody seemed to be both hurrying and waiting at the same time.

"It's going to be a little while," Mom told Bo and me. She held a clipboard with a giant stack of papers on top. "I have to figure out some insurance stuff. Are you two okay?"

I nodded, and Bo did too. He had paper and crayons so he was good to go. And there was some writing I really needed to do, and what better place to do it than in a hospital, where everything began.

My notebook was mostly full, so I flipped to one of the final blank pages. But before I started writing there, I turned to the story Mrs. Yang had read . . . and I crossed it all out.

Revision didn't always mean starting over. A lot of the time it meant changing and improving what you already had. But right now I didn't just want to switch a word or sentence here and there. I wanted to change the whole story.

Sometimes healthy dads fall down, I wrote.

People who were so sure they were right can realize that they're wrong.

They can say sorry. Then—because sorry isn't usually enough all by itself—they can make it right.

Jade hadn't been fair to Zoe, not at all. She'd felt like Zoe was getting out of control, when really Zoe was finding control. She was becoming her own person—something everybody should get to do.

Just like anyone and everyone, Zoe deserved to share her ideas, thoughts, and opinions. She deserved to have dreams and go for them. She deserved to have friends, family, and the right to decide for herself when and where they all hung out. If Zoe wanted a family, she should have one. If she wanted to go somewhere—like to Denver, or the Grand Canyon, or the moon, she should go.

Jade didn't want to control Zoe anymore. She didn't want to worry about what Zoe was doing or thinking back home. She wanted Zoe to do or think whatever she wanted. And if Zoe decided she wanted a different best friend, or to become someone who didn't get along with Jade at all, well, then that's how it would be.

As long as Zoe was being true to herself, that was all Jade could ask. No matter what happened, Jade knew she'd be okay.

≈

I closed my notebook and checked out what was happening around me. There'd been a lot of noise a second ago, and now I realized it was because all our friends from the trip had shown up. Fallan was already playing with Bo, Clue sat down beside me, and all the adults were crowded around Mom.

I smiled to myself. This hospital was so similar to the one we went to the day of Nessa's party. But this time, I didn't feel alone at all.

"I decided to stop controlling Zoe," I told Clue. "I just wrote about it. From here on out, all her decisions are going to be totally her own. She can do literally anything she wants."

Clue nodded, but he seemed distracted.

"We can still try again when we get home," I added. "There must be a way to have them both here. And if there's not . . ." I took a slow breath. "I mean, I'd want to talk to Zoe about it first, but I'd understand if you needed to send her away to bring back Harper. At least until we figure out how to get them both."

"Well, that's the thing," he said. "I don't think I'm going to try again."

"What?"

He chuckled. "Well, while you have been writing about letting go of Zoe, I've been doing the same thing with Harper. I mean, I'm always going to think about her and our memories. But maybe . . . maybe it didn't work for a reason, you know? Maybe she'd want me to focus on who's around me now. I've never really had a best friend besides her. I think she'd be glad that I found one." He shrugged. "And that her magic was a little different than I'd expected."

I blinked. A best friend? Did he mean . . .

Clue elbowed me in the side. "Yeah, you, weirdo. Even though you're horrible at splashing contests."

"*I WASN'T EVEN IN THE POOL!*" I said for the millionth time. "I didn't have my swimsuit on. It was totally unfair!" And then I let out a big, real laugh. I didn't know how Dad's blood was doing, but mine was wide-awake. All of me was. Because the idea of Clue as my best friend . . . well, it sounded pretty good. But there was one thing I was afraid of.

"What if you move?" I asked him.

"What if *you* move?"

We looked at each other for what felt like centuries, but in that time, an interesting thought flashed through my mind. With a friend like Clue, if someone moved . . . would a little distance really be able to keep us apart?

Clue seemed to read my mind. "If someone moves, we stay friends. No matter what. I mean it."

"We could write to each other," I said.

"We do like to write a lot," he joked.

I chuckled.

"You know, I actually sort of miss Tiveda." He sighed.

I thought of our little town. Sure, it wasn't a fancy place. There weren't tall buildings or big parks or malls with more than three stores. And people left. People left all the time. But maybe, by focusing so much on that, I'd forgotten to appreciate where I was, what I had. Our town gave Clue special memories of Harper. It gave me memories with Zoe. It gave us the pond that brought my words to life—and a whole new friendship I never expected.

"Yeah," I agreed. "I miss Tiveda too."

In fact, I couldn't wait to go back.

34
Back Home

Monday night we were back home in Tiveda. We'd barely unpacked when I asked Mom something that'd been on my mind the whole flight back.

"Can I go to the pond with Clue and Zoe for a little bit?"

She looked me up and down and pulled Dad's blanket up to his chin. He was supposed to take it easy the next few days—no more laps up and down any more canyons—so he was back in his chair like before.

"You know I don't like you going there," she said.

I groaned. "I know. But it's important."

Mom put a hand on her hip.

"I don't like it, Jade. I want to keep you safe and healthy. I think that's reasonable."

My eyes narrowed. That was a pretty typical thing for a mom to want, but at the same time . . . "You told us to deal with stuff on our own, remember? To basically look out for ourselves? So which is it? Are you in charge of me or am I?"

Mom made a face like she'd taken a big gulp of bad milk. Then she leaned against the wall.

"When I told you that, I was scared," she said. "I didn't mean for you to keep things from us, or to feel like you needed to take care of *everything* on your own."

I gave that a second to sink in.

"It's cool," I finally said, "but maybe I can actually take care of myself. At least sometimes."

Mom smiled. "I have no doubt that you can." She stood up straighter. "You know what? Go to the pond. Just don't drink the water."

"I promise to keep my mouth closed," I told her. "But not in life. Just at the pond."

Mom laughed and flashed me a thumbs-up. "Deal."

≈

Zoe and I walked to the pond quietly. I couldn't stop staring at her. Since I'd let go of control yesterday, she'd chopped off most of her hair. Now, it only came to her chin—and it was *blue*.

"Do you like it?" she finally asked.

I smiled. "Do *you* like it?"

She hesitated, but then did a little twirl. "I love it," she said.

"Then that's all that matters. But yeah," I said, "I think it's amazing."

When we turned the corner to the pond, Clue was already there, sitting on a rock near the edge. He waved.

"Cool hair, Zoe," he said.

She skipped up to him. "Thanks!" Zoe made a face at the pond. "So creepy," she said. "I wish it was clean enough to swim in."

I raised my eyebrows. "You like swimming?"

She raised hers back. "Heck yes!"

We all watched the murky water. "Well, there are a lot of places you can do it," I told her. "Not here. But there are lots of swimming pools in the world. Lakes too. And oceans."

"What's an ocean?" She wanted to know.

Clue and I exchanged a look as Zoe sat on a rock.

Her eyes gazed well beyond the pond. I closed my eyes and listened to the water, the trees, my town, and the soft breaths of my friends beside me.

I opened to the back cover of my notebook, to the very end of my new story. And I wrote the words I wanted to write here, in Tiveda, by the pond that brought us all together.

Stay or go. It was all up to Zoe.

Once it started to get dark, Zoe and I said bye to Clue and walked back to her house. Along the way I noticed some flowers that weren't actually that dead looking. And my lawn and Zoe's were looking a little greener.

"Goodnight, Zoe," I said, giving her the biggest bear hug I've ever given anyone.

"Goodnight, Jade!" she said, as happy as ever.

35
The Poem

The first thing I noticed on Tuesday morning was Zoe's mailbox.

It was like any other—plain black. No decorations. No stickers. No anything.

I'd kind of known it was coming but that didn't stop the gasp from escaping my mouth. I squeezed Bo's hand, and together we raced across the street. I knocked on the door, but there was no answer. I peeked in the window. The house was dark, and the random assortment of objects, plus the furniture I'd added in later—that was all gone too.

That's when I noticed the folded piece of notebook paper stuck to her front door. It had my name on the front.

I swallowed hard and carefully opened it. Then, I took a deep breath and started to read.

Imperfectly Me
By Zoe Spumoni

I am an idea.
And full of ideas.
Ideas that come from a friend.
She knows me
And would never lead me wrong.
But maybe
I am my ideas too.
I am my likes
Dislikes, opinions,
thoughts, fears.
Wishes, hopes.
Dreams
And
Everything else.
She taught me this
And that the world is mine

To explore
However scary
Confusing and
Up and down it might be.
I can get to know it
As I get to know me.

I am a story
A story of me and my friend.
Talking, laughing, singing, dancing
I am my story
And I'm learning to tell it.
Me
In my
Ever-changing ways.
And I'm starting to think
The best ideas
The best stories or
Songs or
Games or
Adventures
Are the ones
That aren't
Exactly
Perfect.

The edges of my eyes filled with tears, but I laughed to myself too. A poem! She'd written a poem. I guess I'd always imagined that if Zoe wrote something, it'd be stories, like me. But just like she had her own unique thoughts, she had her own way of expressing them too.

I stared at the poem. Held it in my hands carefully as if it were a piece of treasure. Because it was.

Bo squeezed my hand. "Jadey, let's keep going," he said.

I squeezed back. "Okay, buddy," I said. "Let's."

36
The Return of Gresham

Real-Life Zoe hadn't been with me that long, but it still felt weird going to school without her. I wandered through my morning classes in a strange happy-sad daze. Zoe was gone. But somehow, I knew it was the best thing for both of us.

Part of me expected to find an empty table at lunch. But when I rounded the corner to the cafeteria and spotted where I usually sat, there was Clue. And he wasn't alone.

Because the Sparkles were sitting there too.

I shot Clue a look, but he just shrugged.

"Hey," Afiya said.

"Hey," I said.

"I haven't seen Zoe all day. Did she move?"

I nodded slowly. "Yeah, probably. Is that why you're sitting here? To ask me about Zoe?"

"Well, yeah," she said. "But also because if she did move, we thought you might be a little lonely."

The rest of the Sparkles nodded.

"That's how you found me, remember?" Scarlett asked. "When my best friend moved last year, I was sitting at a lunch table staring out into space. But then Afiya and Maggie asked me to sit with them."

"And then we picked up Esme," Afiya added after a second. "And then Camila and then Janelle."

I scratched my head kind of hard. Wait. The Sparkle Girls weren't just together because they liked sparkly things? They were a group who'd all lost their best friends.

"Why did you never ask me?" I wondered out loud.

Afiya shrugged. "You always looked so busy," she said, "or just not interested."

"Yeah," I murmured. "I guess I did." I tucked some hair behind my ears. "Well, I think I'm going to have a lot of free time starting now," I said. "Are you going to be able to finish your health project by yourself, Afiya? I can help, if you want."

She smiled. "That would be great, if you don't mind. And you guys, oh my gosh, I heard from my sister that we're learning about hygiene during our next unit. What if Mr. Kremen brings in some deodorant for us to eat?"

Everybody laughed and eww-ed.

"It might not stink," Clue said. We all groaned.

I leaned back as everybody kept talking. There wasn't really anything special about this lunch. We weren't making paper birds with faces or singing songs like they were written for us alone. We weren't promising to always agree and only ever hang out with each other.

And yet, it felt just right.

When the bell rang to go to class, we passed Mrs. Yang in the hall.

"Word count?" she asked me.

"Umm." I motioned for everyone to go ahead. "I don't know if I'm really going to write at lunch much anymore," I told her. "I think I might be busy."

Mrs. Yang leaned down to meet my gaze, and I realized I was staring at my shoes.

"That's totally okay," she said. "Writing can be part of your life. It shouldn't be the whole thing."

I lifted my head and locked eyes with my teacher for the first time in a little too long.

"Oh, and by the way," I said, "I have a revision I want to show you later, if that's okay. I know it's not my final draft, but I think it's heading in the right direction."

She smiled. "I can't wait to read it."

"Thanks, Mrs. Yang," I said, "for everything." Then I hurried to catch up with my friends.

≈

On Friday Clue and I presented our liver project.

"For the first part of our presentation," I said, "Everyone has to eat some chopped liver."

"Just kidding," Clue added as we watched everyone's freaked-out faces quickly turn to relief.

Next Clue handed out the brochures of information we'd worked on. We read the facts to the class and talked about how important and powerful livers could be. They broke down bad blood cells, made new proteins and energy, and helped medicine work better. There was a lot they could do for you, but you had to make smart, healthy decisions so they could do their jobs.

The last part of our presentation was a game, so people could be involved and Mr. Kremen could make sure they had learned things. People hardly raised their hands, so Clue acted out clues for all the answers, of course.

I nudged him. "They probably shouldn't have help with this."

"Oh," he said. "Yeah, I guess you're right." Then he stopped pretending to make bile, which was good, because he was acting kind of gross.

"Why do you give out clues, anyway?" I asked as we packed up after class.

"Oh, it's something I started doing after Harper died," he said.

We walked into the hall together. "Why?"

His cheeks flushed. "I just thought it might help me . . . I don't know . . . get some friends or something."

I raised my eyebrows. "How'd that work out?"

"I got some. But they were no Jade Levy."

"Maybe it's time to make people come up with answers themselves," I said.

Clue smiled. "Maybe it is. I kind of miss my real name too."

I tested it out. "Gresham," I said. It sounded cool, so I said it again.

"Want to do something later today, Gresham?" I asked.

"Library?"

"Mall?"

"Pond?"

We grinned at each other.

"We'll figure it out," I said.

"Sounds good," said Gresham.

We waved at each other, and then went our separate ways to our next classes.

37
My Story

When we got home later, Bo and I went straight to Dad's chair.

"How are my three favorite kids this afternoon?" he greeted us.

"Two," I corrected with a smile.

He raised his eyebrows, because he finally had them again. They were thin, but they were totally there. "Two?"

"Yeah." I sat on the armrest of his chair. "Zoe moved away. And I don't think I'm going to go back to writing about my other Zoe anymore, if that's okay with you. I didn't realize it until recently, but I have a lot of other ideas I want to explore. Like maybe there's a group of friends who go around rescuing kids who don't have best friends. I also want to work on this series about people who take care of towns that really need their help."

I bit my lip. Maybe I shouldn't have blurted all that out. Maybe Dad needed me to keep writing about Zoe. He was better now, but the trip had proven that maybe there were still going to be some bumps in the road.

"I'm going to miss friend Zoe and fictional Zoe," he said. "But those sound like super-duper spectacular new ideas to me."

I sighed. "Yeah, but Zoe helps you get better."

Dad pulled me closer to him. "*You* help me get better," he said. "Cancer is a tricky thing. Sometimes you're fine and then there comes a little not-fine surprise, like with anything in life. But you know what helps me get through it? Your positive attitude, your endless imagination, and your strong spirit."

I blushed. "I did write one last thing sort of about Zoe," I said. "Do you want to hear it?"

"Do I want to hear it?" he repeated. "Is spiky love the best love?"

That seemed like a yes. So I cleared my throat and pulled out my notebook.

Part of me felt nervous, sharing this story with Dad. For some reason it felt scarier than any of my others. I wondered if it had something to do with the fact that I'd really taken Mrs. Yang's advice to heart with this one. I'd revised and made it the best it could be. It could probably be better still, but I'd done the best I could right now, and that made me feel proud. Really proud.

I started to read.

THE THING ABOUT OPPOSITES
By Jade Levy

The thing about opposites is that sometimes the ones that seem the most obvious aren't actually opposites at all. Like real and fake. They seem as different as can be, but they're not. Real people can act fake, sometimes, and fake people can become real.

There was once a girl named Zoe, who was fake— or made up—until she became real. Once there was a girl named Jade, who wasn't much different. Jade was a faker because she didn't act real. She didn't admit that she was scared of things like her best friend not liking her and losing her dad.

So, in her little room in her little house in her little town, she wrote a perfect friendship, but it wasn't perfect at all. It wasn't even a friendship. When friends didn't trust each other, talk to each other, or give each other the freedom to be themselves, it was actually the opposite of friendship. And she didn't write about her dad at all. Maybe, Jade realized, the scariest things to write were the things that needed writing the most. She'd keep writing fiction, of course. But maybe she'd write about her dad too. And about herself. And hard feelings. She could do all this now . . . now that she had set Zoe free.

My voice was getting wobbly, so maybe it was time to stop reading out loud. As I went to hand Dad my notebook, it wiggled in my grip just the slightest bit. It was like something or someone was alive in there, pushing it up, pushing it forward.

"Zoe?" I whispered extra-soft.

My notebook didn't say anything back, but I knew what the answer was.

"Everything okay?" Dad asked. "I'd love to hear more."

"Sure thing," I said. "Here. You can read the rest for yourself."

I squeezed the notebook to my chest one last time.

And then I let go.

Acknowledgments

OPPSERVATION: Many people think writing a book is a one-person job. After all, there's only one name on the cover! But creating a book like *Friend or Fiction* actually takes a big, wonderful team.

Questions for further research: Who else played a part?

We'll start with my editor, Julie Bliven, who saw the potential in this story and knew exactly what I could do to make it stronger in each and every round of revision. I am so grateful for her feedback, support, and friendship throughout this process. I'm thankful for everyone at Charlesbridge, including Donna Spurlock, Meg Quinn, Jordan Standridge, and Mel Schuit in Marketing, and Art Director Diane Earley. Another huge thank-you goes out to copyeditor Bridget McCaffrey, proofreader Emily Mitchell, and to the amazing cover artist Julie McLaughlin. There is nothing fictional about how fantastic I think you all are!

Thank you to my wonderful agent, Rebecca Sherman, as well as Andrea Morrison, Allie Levick, and everyone at Writers House. Thank you for believing in this story and in me.

This book went through many, many drafts, and it would not be what it is now without my incredible early readers. Endless thanks to Kalvin Nguyen, Gail Nall, Erika David, Ronni Arno, Jeff Chen, and Dana Edwards for their feedback, and to Lee Gjertsen Malone, Laura Shovan, Vanessa Yudell, Dusti Bowling, Evan Nothmann, and Jenn Bishop (aka my Wise Owl) for helping with a few specific questions along the way.

Thank you writer friends, particularly the Guild, the MG Beta Readers, and the Sweet Sixteens. It's so great to be able to share the writing and publishing journey with such supportive communities.

Shout-out to all the teachers, librarians, booksellers, and bloggers who connect kids with books, especially my friends from Nerd Camp. Thank you for working so hard to spread the joy of reading. I truly believe that kids who read grow into thoughtful, intelligent, empathetic adults, and by introducing them to books they love, you are making the world a better place. And to the kids I've been fortunate enough to connect with over Skype and in real life: Hi! You're awesome! Keep reading! (And to those I haven't met yet: Hi! You're also awesome! Keep reading!)

Thanks to my family, especially the Sterns, the Baills, and the Rivkins, and to AJ, Rena, and Moreau. I really appreciate that you're always there for me, and that you don't get mad when I disappear to hang out with fictional characters instead of you. And to ALL the people I've been lucky enough to call friends at any point in my life, thank you. As Jade learns, true friendship is wonderful, but it can also be complex, and sometimes people lose touch or grow in different directions. Regardless of where we are in our friendship right now, I'm so grateful for every person with whom I've ever developed that special bond.

I got the idea for this book in part from my parents, Kathy and David Cooper. Not only are they the most supportive people in my world (and possibly the *entire* world), they are also some of the strongest. They've taught me so much about overcoming obstacles, and have proven time and time again that with courage, a positive attitude, and plenty of humor you can get through anything life throws your way.

And to Michael, the ultimate best friend. I am so lucky to have someone by my side who encourages, challenges, supports, pushes, and loves the way you do. Best friends for life.